A Long Way Home

A Sweet Contemporary Gay Romance

Blake Allwood

Blake Allwood Publishing

CONTENT WARNINGS

These topics are discussed, but not explicit:
Homophobia
Death
Loss of Family Member
Orphaned Children
Trauma
Fear of Loss
Recovery
Depression
Murder

Join Blake's email list to get advance notice of new books and receive his occasional newsletter:

www.blakeallwood.com

MM Romance By Blake Allwood	Romantic Fantasy By Adam J. Ridley
Transitions Series Aiden Inspired Suzie Empowered (MF Romance) Bobby Transformed	**Big Bend Series** Love's Legacy (1) Love's Heirloom (2) Love's Bequest (3)
Chance Series Love By Chance Another Chance With Love Taking A Chance For Love	**The Witch Brothers Series** Emerald Earth Diamond Air Ruby Fire Sapphire Water
Romantic Series Romantic Renovations (1) Romantic Rescue (2) Romantic Recon (3)	
Melody Series Melody of the Heart Melody of the Snow	
Road to Rocktoberfest Anthology Changing His Tune - 2022	
Coming Home Series (2023) A Long Way Home Family Home Down Home …and many more	
Novellas Tenacious Moon's Place	

ACKNOWLEDGMENTS

Special thanks to the following amazing people who helped me get this book finished and into your hands.

Jo Bird: Editor
Renee Mizar: Editor
Ann Attwood: Proofreader

And of course, a big thank you to my husband who puts up with my endless stories and handles the formatting and final publishing of all my books.

ONE

PROLOGUE

"**O**LIVIA, OLIVIA!" I WHISPER-SHOUTED. "Don't do it! We're gonna get in trouble. Again."

"Shh, you're gonna give us away. Just shut up and keep an eye out."

Olivia snuck down the hall of the old Victorian, and into the master bedroom. She'd found the garter snake under a bush out front while weeding the garden, which we'd been told to do as punishment for some other naughty crime I'd already forgotten.

Olivia slipped into the room while Chase and I kept guard. Why she always left us to stand guard, I'd never understand, as we always got distracted. Meaning, of course, that we *always* got caught.

Sure enough, Mrs. Simmons came out of one of the rooms, and saw Chase and me sitting suspiciously next to the stairs. "And just what are you two doing up here?"

she asked as she looked around. "And more importantly, where is your coconspirator?"

Just then, Olivia came out of the bedroom with a smile the size of the Cheshire cat's. "Oh no, missy," Mrs. Simmons said. "Back in there, and you bring whatever it was you took in back out!"

Olivia looked at Chase and me with disgust. Not a new look, mind you, since we got it almost every time we were in trouble. She turned back into the bedroom, with Mrs. Simmons on her heels.

A second later, we heard a yelp from Mrs. Simmons. Chase and I couldn't help but peek around the corner, only to see Olivia holding the snake up to Mrs. Simmons's face. Our guardian had a look of barely suppressed terror, mixed with a good dose of rage.

Mrs. Simmons was a saint. The three of us knew it, even though we found great pleasure in tormenting her. Despite Olivia still gripping the snake, Mrs. Simmons got ahold of her ear and pulled her along the hallway and down the stairs.

Chase and I followed, but not close enough for Mrs. Simmons to notice us, we hoped. When Mrs. Simmons, the snake, and Olivia's very red ear were all outside, she instructed Olivia to put the slippery reptile back in a cool place, then return to the porch, so she could have a word with us all.

"Boys, you too, all three of you. I want to see you front and center!" Mrs. Simmons had three distinct tones: the *you are funny, but I have to fuss at you anyway* tone, the *I can't believe you did that* tone, and the *you really have gone too far this time* tone. She was using that last one this time.

When we were all gathered on the front porch, sneaking glances at Mrs. Simmons, and trying not to smile or cry, the woman drew in a deep breath, and sighed. "The three of you sit down right where you are standing."

After doing as we were told, Mrs. Simmons sat in a chair and looked at us for a long time. Finally, she shook her head, put her hands in her lap, and slumped forward.

"Children, this morning I went to a doctor's appointment, and was told I have a sickness called multiple sclerosis. They call it MS for short. It means I may no longer be able to take care of you."

The tears streamed down Mrs. Simmons's face for a moment before she was able to compose herself. It was the only time I'd ever seen her lose control, and I knew I'd never forget it.

"I love you three like you were my biological children, even when you're totally naughty." She gave Olivia a very pointed look. "When Charles, um, Mr. Simmons died two years ago, I had to argue with Children's Services that I was still qualified to care for you, but now with my diagnosis, I know they're going to force me to give you up, unless..." She seemed to still herself for a moment, trying to find the right words. "The three of you keep getting in trouble, not just here, but at school, so the state will want to put you in a more... controlled environment. I know you're not bad kids, and I know that you are mostly just mischievous, but things are changing. If I'm going to have any hope of keeping you, I'm going to need your help. I need you to make an effort to *try* to stay out of trouble."

She took another long breath, looking at each of us, then her lean, tall body once again slumped in the chair. It was the first and only time I'd ever seen her let go of her normally perfect piano-teacher posture. The three of us had come to live with the Simmonses when we were still small. Now, we were all pre-teens, and Mrs. Simmons was having an adult conversation with us, one I wasn't prepared to hear.

But, even her serious news couldn't deter Mrs. Simmons from launching into one of her old-fashioned lectures. "I love you with all my heart, and as such, I must tell you that harming another creature is the most inappropriate wrong you can do. Olivia, how do you think that poor snake felt while you were hauling it to my bedroom?" she asked. "What about you, Chase? Would you like someone to grab you out of your comfortable room and throw you somewhere you had never been before? Gib? What about you? Are you able to imagine how scary it would be to lose your home in one quick moment, because someone was inconsiderate enough—" She gave Olivia another pointed look. "—and *mean* enough to kidnap you and throw you somewhere you'd never been?"

Olivia had never looked scared or chastised before, and both Chase and I were concerned when she looked stricken by Mrs. Simmons's words.

"A-Are you gonna die, Mrs. Simmons?" Olivia finally asked.

Mrs. Simmons looked at Olivia with what appeared to be exhaustion mixed with sadness. "We will all die someday, little one," Mrs. Simmons reached down then, and pulled Olivia up and onto her lap. "But, yes, if I don't control the stress in my life, it could cause me to get sick faster."

Mrs. Simmons never threw false punches. She had always been straight with us, never lying or trying to tell us half-truths.

"I'm going to ask my sister Margaret to move in with us... to help out, but she doesn't do well with kids. She even hated being a kid herself." Mrs. Simmons chuckled a little. "So, if you want to stay, you can't be naughty or mischievous when she arrives. You will have to be on your best behavior. I'm afraid if she refuses to help me, the state will come and rehome you with other people."

Olivia was once again stricken. "I always thought you'd adopt us."

The tears began falling down Mrs. Simmons's face again. "Yes, dear one, I thought I was going to adopt you too, but now that I'm sick, they will never let me." She wrapped Olivia into a tighter hug and squeezed her. "But, that is no matter. I don't have to adopt you for you to be mine, do you hear me?"

We all nodded and believed her, because Mrs. Simmons would never lie to us. As Mrs. Simmons had said, her sister was not a fan of children. Miss Margaret Latham was, in every aspect, a Southern Victorian woman transported to the twenty-first century. Her clothing may have been current, but her beliefs about raising and treating children were strictly from an earlier time.

From that point on, the three of us defined our lives as before Miss Margaret and after Miss Margaret. Before, we were free, and life was full of adventure. After, we were full of fear, and always waiting for the day Miss Margaret would send us away.

A house that was at one time loud and full of life was now quiet and death-like. Mrs. Simmons spent more and more time to herself as she slowly became less and less able to control her body or her movements.

The three of us spent our teenage years avoiding getting into trouble. When other teens were experimenting, we were just trying to stay together. There was little room for error in the world of Miss Margaret.

The year we all went to college, each getting a scholarship, because Miss Margaret tolerated nothing less than perfect grades, Mrs. Simmons was permanently placed in assisted living. She was only thirty-nine.

All three of us took turns going to see her, but her MS was aggressive, and it took her from us just three years later. It was the end of our junior year of college, and the grief almost consumed us.

We buried Mrs. Ruby Simmons next to her husband in the church graveyard. After the funeral, we went back to the house, which was packed to the rafters with mourners. The love we felt for Mrs. Simmons was not reserved only for us. Our entire small, rural, West Tennessee town seemed to love her as well, and I was sure everyone in the county had come either to the service, the funeral, or our home afterward.

When the crowd finally left, we helped the church ladies clean the kitchen, while Miss Margaret sat in the parlor, staring out the window.

After everyone had left, Olivia leaned against the counter, and looked at Chase, then at me. "This probably isn't the time to tell you—" Olivia began, "—but Chase and I are kind of dating."

"Eww," I said, before I could stop myself. "You're like sister and brother."

Olivia laughed. "Well, not really. *You* are like my brother."

Chase agreed. "*You* are like my brother too, but it's always been different between Olivia and me. We always knew we would be more one day."

The pit of my stomach rolled at the thought. Maybe it had been different for them, but I couldn't see it. I managed to swallow it though, and gave my best fake smile.

"That's good, I guess."

Olivia elbowed Chase in the ribs. "I told you he wouldn't be okay with this." Chase just bowed his head, and refused to look me in the eye.

"Listen, Gib, you had a right to know before anyone else, but it's bound to get out now we're not hiding it any longer. We just thought you needed to hear it from us."

I felt like I'd lost my mother and my siblings all at the same time, and the feeling of sickness was becoming harder to control.

"Um... give me a minute," I said, and dashed to the bathroom, where I was no longer able to hold it all down. You know how sometimes you would feel better after you had puked? Well, this wasn't one of those times. I leaned back against the bathroom door and tried to catch my breath.

A second later, I heard a knock on the door. "Gib, buddy?" Chase's voice sounded apologetic. "Miss Margaret wants to speak to us in the parlor. She sent me to come fetch you."

I stood up without responding and washed my face. I wasn't in the mood for one of Miss Margaret's lectures about maintaining my composure.

Chase was gone when I came out, and I assumed he'd joined Miss Margaret in the parlor.

When I entered the room, I noticed Miss Margaret was sitting in the formal Victorian chair no one ever sat in, because it was as painfully uncomfortable as it was ugly. She seemed to fit the chair nicely, though.

When I sat down across from Olivia and Chase, she briefly cocked an eyebrow, noticing I didn't sit with them. We had always been a cohesive unit, especially when facing Miss Margaret, but tonight, I didn't have the strength to join them on the settee.

Miss Margaret was barely holding in her emotions as she spoke. I looked at Olivia and Chase and, despite the new strain on our relationship, we exchanged perplexed looks. We'd never seen Miss Margaret demonstrate anything that resembled emotions other than anger and stoicism.

She drew in a breath, and after slowly letting it out, said, "My sister loved you and she made me swear that you would always have a home here if you needed one. In fact, in her will she stipulated that the house belonged to the three of you, but that I could live here until my death. Of course, I don't need the home, I have my own, so I won't be staying for long."

There was something confusing in her tone. I thought she'd be mad about not inheriting the house, since she'd grown up in it too, but what I heard in her voice sounded more like concern. If I hadn't known this woman so well, I'd have thought her concern was for us, but that wasn't Miss Margaret's way, so I must've misread it.

"She also left the three of you a significant sum of money to be kept in a trust until your twenty-fifth birthdays. At that point, you can either take the money in a lump sum, or monthly installments that should last you your entire lives. It is completely up to you."

Miss Margaret seemed to have finished and the three of us stood to leave, when she said, "Please, wait a moment. I-I…" She stopped talking, emotion taking hold once again.

"My sister isn't the only one who loves you. It's no secret that I didn't want to come here to be your caretaker. I honestly thought I'd be here only as long as my sister needed me, then either we'd send you to boarding school or back to the state." Her tears became more like sobs, but none of us were brave enough to console her. When she finally regained control, she used a tissue to properly wipe away the tears and blow her nose. Even in mourning, she was intensely proper. "It's also no secret that I've never wanted children. Our father was a strict, rigid man. When our mother died, we were stuck with him and I hated him for being a cold, unloving person. I knew I would be just like him, and I swore I'd never put children through that, but after Charles died and Ruby asked if I could come help with the three of you, I decided to try."

She looked at each of us as the tears streamed down her face. Utter shock held me in place as Miss Margaret continued to speak, "I know you hate me, and I don't blame you. I would've hated me too, but despite what you may think, I'm not without feeling. The three of you have filled my life with happiness like I never knew existed." I quickly glanced over at Olivia, whose eyes were wide and filled with her own tears. "I don't deserve your forgiveness, or even your love, but I hope one day you'll understand that I stayed here not out of obligation, or even for Ruby's sake. I stayed because I wanted to help raise you. Ruby said, over and over, there had to be love mixed with the discipline. I figured as long as she was around, she could handle the love, and I could handle the discipline." She looked at the three of us and sighed. "Now you need both, and I'm not sure I can do that." The tears continued to stream down her face, making her look much older than her forty-six years.

We stood there silently, unsure what to say or do. We'd been held captive by her words... words that were quite different from any we thought we'd ever hear from her. None of us could have imagined stern Miss Margaret as being a sensitive, feeling person underneath, let alone that she would tell us she loved us.

As usual, Olivia came to her senses before either Chase or me, and turned to Miss Margaret, took her hand, and said, "We aren't sure what to say, Miss Margaret. You've never made any claims of caring about us before. You may have to give us a little time to digest all this."

Miss Margaret nodded as Olivia leaned back on her heels, still holding Miss Margaret's hand. To this day, I don't know what inspired me to comment, since I usually let Olivia or Chase deal with things, but something about Miss Margaret's confession sparked real emotion in me.

"Miss Margaret," I said. "When I was very young, both my parents died in a car accident, and the rest of my family didn't want me. I ended up going to several homes before Mr. and Mrs. Simmons took me in. The day Mrs. Simmons told us she was sick, and you were coming to help take care of us is etched in my memory. I was sure I was going to lose my family again and I'll never have the words to explain the terror that brought me. I cried every night for a year, expecting the monsters, or Children's Services workers, to come and take me away. When you arrived, I knew you were strong enough to keep the monsters away. I'm not going to lie to you, I was... okay, maybe I still am scared of you, but I thanked God every night after you arrived, and that you were strong enough to protect us."

Chase walked over and joined Olivia on the floor, grabbing Miss Margaret's other hand as I knelt beside them. All of us ended up crying that day. Despite her rigidity, we all knew and understood that if she hadn't come, or more importantly, if she hadn't stayed, we would have lost our family, and nothing she did or didn't do would be as bad as that.

Two

Allen

I DIALED MY FATHER'S number, dreading the conversation.

"Hello?" I heard my half-brother's voice. *Damn*, I thought to myself, *he never answers the landline. Why did he this time?*

"Hey, Lance, is Dad there?"

"No."

I sighed. My brother always made it hard on me if I needed to speak to Dad. Of course, Dad had a mobile phone, but he'd banned me from calling it, saying he paid for a landline, so I should use that unless it was an emergency.

"Lance, when will he be back?" I tried desperately to keep the frustration out of my voice. I needed to reach Dad sooner rather than later.

"I don't know." *God help me, my brother's such a jerk.*

"Then, I need to leave him a message."

I wasn't surprised when the line went dead. I now had no choice but to call Dad's mobile. Inviting my own family to attend what should be one of my proudest accomplishments, graduating from college, shouldn't feel like such a burden.

I plopped down on the sofa in my mom's apartment, and leaned my head back before closing my eyes.

Dad had divorced my mom when I was only seven after cheating on her, then married *the other woman*. The woman wasn't a horrible person, but she'd clearly been a social climber.

They'd met while working together at a prestigious hospital in Queens, New York. My father was the lead surgeon there, and his future wife was the secretary on his unit. Their only child, Lance, was born shortly after.

Lance pretty-much hated me from the time he could talk. Of course, Dad divorced his mom a few months after he was born, so I always felt a bit sorry for him. No matter how he felt about me, I knew he had it worse than I ever would. Lance's mom had given full custody to Dad, then promptly disappeared from their lives. So, Lance had to constantly deal with our father's horrible attitude, while I had an amazing and loving mom who shielded me from the worst of it.

Mom came into the room and asked what was wrong, pulling me out of my thoughts.

"Are you sure you can't come to the family luncheon? I'd rather you were there instead of Dad."

She shook her head. "I tried, honey, but your grandpa said someone from the family needs to cover the meeting with the French hotel we're buying. Like I said, though, I'll fly out that night and be there the next day. I promise not to miss graduation."

She kissed the top of my head as she walked back toward the kitchen.

This wasn't the first time our family's hotel business had taken priority. Mom had temporarily taken over the CEO position after Grandpa suffered a mild stroke, and she'd always been his right-hand person in the company anyway.

I'd recently overheard Mom talking with Grandpa on the phone about selling the company, but they must've decided against it. My being accepted into Harvard Medical School in the fall rather than joining the business probably factored into that.

Ultimately, I thought her biggest issue wasn't with me going into medicine, or anything to do with me at all. She'd blamed all her relationship problems with Dad on his career. I had to confess that even though Dad drove me insane, I'd always admired him for what he did for a living.

It's funny, because when I'd told him I was going into pre-med, he just said, "You'll have to get your grades up." *My father's a total asshole.* So, it was no wonder I dreaded inviting him to my graduation events.

At least he'd shown a hint of emotion at my acceptance to Harvard. Fortunately, I no longer cared what he thought, or sought his approval. I got into Harvard on my own academic merits, rather than relying on his connections, or my privileged background, and that alone should make any parent proud. None of it made picking up the phone to call him any easier, though.

I silently kicked my feet out in frustration as soon as Mom was out of sight, grabbed my phone, and dialed his stupid mobile. *God, why does everything have to be so freaking difficult?*

Three

Gib

I'D NEVER FORGIVEN CHASE and Olivia for being together. I considered them my sister and brother, and when their relationship turned romantic, I took that as a betrayal of everything we'd had as children.

It was the Fourth of July when I confessed to them that I'd been accepted into Harvard.

"So, I have news," I said as we sat together on the same old blanket we'd used since we were little kids. When I had their attention, I continued, "I've been accepted into Harvard Medical School."

"Are you going to go?" Chase asked.

I nodded, then stared up toward the sky as the fireworks began. There was a theme with us that we never picked the right times to share difficult news. As the fireworks exploded overhead, Olivia cried, and Chase's face took on a sick look.

"Are you leaving because of us?" Olivia asked once the show ended.

The truth was, absolutely, but, of course, I couldn't say that. "No," I said instead. "This is just a really great opportunity. And guess what? You'll never believe this, but Miss Margaret even volunteered to pay for my education." That seemed to alleviate some of the tension as both Olivia and Chase stared at me in disbelief.

"You've got to be kidding me," Olivia said.

For a brief moment, we were children again, and I shrugged before we collapsed into fits of laughter, trying to reconcile the woman who raised us and the charitable woman who had only admitted she loved us a year before.

"We also have news," Olivia said. Once again, the wall between us came back up, and I cringed inside as I prepared to hear what I already knew was coming.

Olivia, of course, detected my mood change, but ignored it. Another tear did manage to escape down her face, though, which I saw and regretted. Finally, she shook off the sadness and smiled, saying, "We're engaged."

I smiled, but knew they could tell it was forced. The two looked at each other again, exchanging unspoken dialogue I no longer shared with them. Clearly, there was more to tell, and I wasn't at all sure I was ready to hear it. I'd managed to ignore their relationship this past year, able to say at least to myself that it would pass, but now they were engaged... and there was more news.

That *more* meant things would never go back to how they had been... back when we were all a family.

After we gathered up our picnic supplies and began walking toward the old Victorian, Chase said, "There's more." His eyes never left Olivia, and it was plain as day they really were in love. I felt like an ass for not being able to accept it, but the feeling of betrayal still held tight to my heart. Chase cleared his throat as he looked over at me, then back to the ground. "We're pregnant," he said. Neither of them smiled or tried to ease the awkwardness of the situation. We had known and loved each other too long for that.

I sighed, before asking, "Have you told Miss Margaret?"

I could see the two of them exchange sad looks, before answering, "We've told her we're getting married, but not about the baby. She'll have a hard time with the pregnancy, so we're going to tell her about the baby *after* we're married."

I looked out over the dispersing crowd as the noise of the celebrations drifted around us.

When I turned back toward them, Olivia was leaning into Chase, and they were both looking at anything *but* me.

Olivia was the first to break the silence. "We never planned to fall in love, Gib, it just happened. In fact, we've been in love for a very long time. We both decided to hide it from you, because we knew you'd never be okay with it. After we started college, I knew it was time to come clean. I didn't want you to find out through gossip. It was insensitive to tell you when I did, though."

I shrugged, not knowing what to say. Only after we were approaching the home we'd all grown up in, did I stop and turn toward them. "I don't get it. I don't think I ever will, because like I said, you're my siblings, and I never thought of you as anything else. I won't pretend that doesn't hurt, because it does," I said, knowing I was pushing some of my hurt back on them.

Not ready to go inside, we all sat on the steps of the huge porch for several moments before I broke the silence. "I love you and always will. I'm sure we'll eventually work this out, but you have to give me time. When is the wedding?" I asked, not really wanting to know.

"We want to get it done before I start to show, so in a couple months... the plan is September, over Labor Day weekend."

"Where are you getting married?" I asked, becoming more curious.

Olivia looked back toward the old home, not wanting to say anything Miss Margaret might overhear. Luckily for them, she wouldn't be back for another hour or so. Seeing the house was empty, Olivia continued.

"Miss Margaret said we should use the house. It won't be a big crowd, just a few of our friends and some of the folks from church. Pastor Jones has already agreed to do the ceremony. We really want you there. Will you stand up with us?" Olivia asked.

I inwardly sighed, but nodded. They were my family, my only family. I wouldn't let them down, no matter how much of an issue I had with what they were doing... what they'd already done.

"Of course," I barely got out before Olivia and Chase pulled me into a big group hug.

Needless to say, I was more than happy to escape West Tennessee and my complicated family. Harvard would be tough, but it didn't hold a candle to my home life.

FOUR

ALLEN

I LOOKED OVER AT my pompous father and his new wife, Kassidy, and once again, I asked myself why I'd felt obligated to invite him to my graduation luncheon. Despite the happy families surrounding us talking about the exciting futures ahead, the mood at our table was tense, to say the freaking least.

"Where's Lance?" I asked, when Dad and Kassidy picked me up from Mom's place.

"He didn't want to come." I could hear all the loaded crap in that statement, but chose not to take the bait. Dad often liked pitting the two of us against each other.

"Well, I appreciate you coming," I said, trying to keep the sarcasm out of my voice.

We rode in silence all the way to the luncheon and probably stood out like a sore thumb among the crowd of happy people waiting to be seated.

I shook my head slightly when I caught a glimpse of Kassidy. I could tell my very elegantly dressed new step-mother was trying to make the best of a very awkward situation. She and Dad had gotten married just a few months before, and the fact that she was less than three years older than me felt... well, freaking strange, quite frankly.

Even though I didn't want to, I couldn't help but like her. Kassidy was bright and funny, and most importantly, she didn't put up with any crap from my dad. That was admirable if nothing else was.

No surprise, Dad spent the afternoon speaking to everyone except me. Luckily, we'd been seated with the family of a woman I'd had classes with, so I could chat with her instead of staring into space bored out of my head.

On the drive back to Mom's, Dad asked if I was dating the woman. Of course, I stared at him as if he'd just grown horns.

"Dad, I'm gay," I deadpanned.

How could he not already know that? I'd come out to Mom when I was fourteen. I just figured she'd told him, since she told him everything else about me that she deemed important enough for him to know.

Dad cleared his throat, then nodded before pulling up to Mom's brownstone.

"That's it?" I asked, feeling a need to clear the air before getting out of the car.

"What else do you want?" he asked. I could hear the peeved note in his voice.

I shook my head. "Dad, you're a piece of work. So, does this mean I need to find alternative funding for medical school?"

The subject of Dad paying for my education never sat easily with me. I preferred to make my own way, and I'd earned a full-ride academic scholarship for my undergraduate studies. I figured I'd get loans to pay for medical school, and knew Mom would help if I asked her, but Dad shocked me when he'd offered to fund it all himself. I should've known nothing came that easy with him. Kassidy turned toward my father, then looked at me in the backseat. Without waiting for him to answer my question, she said, "No, your sexuality is your own business, and *we* will be happy to pay for your education. Isn't that right, Evan?"

My father looked shocked, but quickly nodded and turned back to face the road. If I hadn't already liked Kassidy, I did now. Had Kassidy not intervened, I was sure our conversation would've ended much worse than it did.

I stepped out of the car, but before they pulled away, I mouthed, "Thank you," where Dad couldn't see. Kassidy smiled and winked at me just as Dad pulled back into the traffic and they disappeared down the road.

FIVE

GIB

I SAT ON THE lonely bench nestled in the trees, ignoring the coolness of the air. I loved spending time in the small hidden alcove when I wasn't in class. The other students bustled around me, but unless they looked straight at me, they rarely knew I was there.

My classes were hard. I knew they would be, of course, but knowing and experiencing were two very different things. The university I'd gone to for pre-med had done absolutely nothing to prepare me for Harvard Medical School.

As I hefted my monster textbook onto my lap, regretting my decision to buy a real book, instead of using the e-book option most of my classmates used. I noticed two men making out across from me. Either they couldn't see me, or didn't care, and I was trying not to be too much of a perv by staring, but even now, seeing two handsome guys kissing and in public sent chills through my body.

I took a deep breath and let it out slowly as I tore my gaze away. *That's never going to be me.* Even if by some miracle someone decided they liked me, I doubted I'd ever feel comfortable with PDAs like those two men.

I'd always known I was gay, long before I ever acknowledged it to anyone, myself included. Growing up in a conservative, small Southern town, being out wasn't really a viable option. I also knew as long as I stayed there, it was unlikely I'd ever have a long-term relationship with anyone. One of my hopes in attending Harvard, before I'd actually experienced it at least, was that maybe I'd find love here. My hopes had yet to materialize in the form of a man, though.

Other than hooking up with the occasional stranger, I hadn't made any friends during undergraduate school either, and mostly just studied and kept to myself, exactly like I was doing now at Harvard. Seeing men openly kissing and holding hands here on campus felt liberating, but also made me feel even lonelier.

I flipped my textbook closed and forced the monster into my already overpacked bookbag.

I quickly glanced over at the two kissing men and sighed inwardly. No, I'd never have that. I was pathetically shy and missed my siblings, although I couldn't really call them that anymore, could I? It was bad enough that everyone on campus probably thought I was a redneck, because I spoke with a Southern twang. If they knew the two people I'd grown up with and considered my brother and sister were now married and had a kid, well, that would pretty much stick a fork in what was left of my reputation.

I missed Olivia and Chase so much sometimes, it hurt. We'd never been far away from each other before. In high school and college, the other kids thought we were cliquish and pretty much avoided us anyway, because Olivia was a bit of an overly protective jerk. I just didn't think they understood what it was like being foster children who, at any moment, could lose everything that meant anything to us, including each other.

The alarm on my phone went off, pulling me from my thoughts, and telling me it was time to go to class.

I arrived early enough to sit near the front. I was easily distracted, and sitting in the back didn't help, so I made a point of getting to all my classes early to grab a prime seat.

"Today, students," our elderly professor said, looking as if he could drop dead at any moment, "I will pair you up with partners for this course. Make sure you combine your schedules, because your grade will depend on how well each of you perform."

I sighed. I hated group participation. I always seemed to get stuck with a lazy partner, and more often than not, my grades suffered when they couldn't or wouldn't pull their weight.

Gibbon Ridley, you will be paired with Alexi Jones. I looked up just in time to see a beautiful woman, also sitting in the front, stand and walk toward me. Her smile was bright, and it lightened my sour attitude. Before I knew it, I was smiling back at her.

"Gib," I said, when she shook my outstretched hand.

"Alexi," she replied. "Hope you like studying."

I prefer it to failing!" I said, letting the smart-ass side of me slip out.

Instead of offending her, she literally laughed out loud, causing several other students to look over at us.

She blushed a bit before smiling again. "I think we're going to get along fine."

That afternoon, as I met Alexi in her dorm room, she introduced me to her friends Fiona and Allen. The three were intense, to say the least.

As they rambled on about several topics at once, Alexi must've noticed me staring with a look of surprise and maybe a little envy. "I'm sorry, Gib," she said. "We've known each other since we were kids. We can be a bit much."

I laughed. "I have siblings and we're the same way. Trust me, I get it."

The three welcomed me into their world after that. Apparently, no one wanted to spend time with them, because they were kooky and loud and didn't give a damn what everyone else thought.

Even though Alexi and I were officially paired together for the entire semester, we were all in med school together, and the three friends came as a package deal, so that is how I became one of the Apple Fritter Gang. The name was a take-off of an old nineteen seventies film called *The Apple Dumpling Gang*. The moniker didn't hold much meaning other than cause one of us to pick up apple fritters once a week from the bakery just off campus, which was a perk we all enjoyed.

It wasn't long before the four of us became inseparable. We really were our own gang, if you could call a small group of geeky med students who studied more than partied a gang. For the first time since my relationship with Olivia and Chase had shifted, I felt like I had people who just got me.

Six

Allen

D REAMY, DROP-DEAD GORGEOUS. I couldn't breathe.

Gib Ridley was tall, at least six foot three. Beautiful dusty-blond hair fell across his forehead, longer than it should've been, but still suiting his handsome face. He had an air about him that said controlled and well put together. I wanted to take him apart the moment we met, and that was before hearing his sexy-as-hell Southern accent.

I turned into a blubbering idiot whenever I was around Gib, and continued to flirt with him as if my life depended on it. Unfortunately, the guy was clueless. *Fuck*, I thought, *he's straight. I finally meet a man who ticks all my boxes, and he's fucking straight.*

I resigned myself to my secret crush. Over the weeks I watched him, getting to know him as a friend, and hoping against hope he was gay, and maybe I had a chance. Gib was quiet, but not what I'd call shy, to say nothing of his occasional dark expressions and contemplative brooding. He was more of a take me or leave me kind of guy. There was also something about the way he held himself, almost like he was a proper Southern gentleman from another time. Of course, that pushed all my buttons.

It took a long time to fully break the ice with Gib. He was friendly, but guarded, and wasn't forthcoming about his family or background. We knew he didn't have a scholarship, so he must come from money, but nothing about him seemed to convey that.

I doubted Gib ever worried what others thought, and for that, I was really jealous. I might have been out and proud, but I still obsessed about how I looked, how I moved, and if I was being too femme, or not femme enough. I was a total queen, and I knew it.

After the first month secretly pining for Gib, I'd had enough. I needed help figuring this out, or I was going to drive myself mad. "Alexi, help!" I finally asked, when we were alone together.

"Help what?" she asked as she started the coffee machine I kept in my room.

"Is he gay? I have to know!"

Alexi looked at me knowingly, and asked, "Who?"

"Ugh, you're such a bitch! You *know* who."

Alexi just smirked. "Here's a clue, you've literally thrown yourself at the guy since you met him. He's not made any moves, right?"

I sighed and lay back on my bed. "That doesn't mean he's not gay. He could just be shy."

Alexi laughed out loud. "Listen, if it'll make you feel better, we'll find out."

I jumped off my bed and grabbed Alexi in a bear hug, nearly causing her to drop her coffee. "You're the best friend ever!" I exclaimed. She just shook her head.

SEVEN

GIB

"**G**AY OR STRAIGHT?" ALEXI asked as she watched the same two guys I'd seen kissing the day I met her. The men were having a lover's spat just a few feet from us.

"Um, what?" I asked.

"Gay or straight?" she repeated, like she had some right to know.

"Does it matter?" I asked, feeling a bit defensive about my new friend apparently trying to out me.

"No, it doesn't, but the way you were leering at those two guys makes me think you're at least bisexual."

I shook my head. "It's not a secret and not that it matters, 'cause I never date or even hook up, but I'm attracted to men."

"I knew it!" Alexi said, and hugged me. "I like women more than men, and I knew you were family."

I laughed. "What the hell? Family?"

"Oh yeah, it means you're LGBTQ+."

I shrugged. "Like I said, I don't really act on my sexuality, so at the moment, I'm more asexual. Not that I want to be, it's just I'm never going to be one of those guys who can screw around with someone I'm not attached to."

"Oh, that's not asexual, that's more demisexual," she said. "You only prefer people you have a relationship with."

I shrugged again, although I did like learning there was actually a term for how I felt. I was still the same as I'd always been, regardless of labels.

"Anyway," Alexi said, "I could fix you up with some people if you're interested."

"God, no!" I said, putting my hands up in front of my face. "This demisexual thing, I'm almost sure that means no blind dates! Absolutely none!"

Alexi laughed, and just like that, my sexuality was off the discussion table, although I was still more than a little confused why it came up to begin with.

EIGHT

ALLEN

WITH ALEXI'S HELP, I finally knew that Gib liked guys. Still, no matter what I did, he never showed any interest, not even when I all but attacked him one night, pretending to be drunk.

Granted, I shouldn't have expected anything less than chivalry from him, but I was getting desperate. I only drank a few shots, enough to give me a buzz, then I put on the drunk act. I admit I'd done it with closeted boys in the past, and it tended to work like a charm, but that wasn't the case with Gib.

"Gib, I drank too much to go home. It's too far. I'm gonna crash with you tonight." I intentionally slurred my words to sound the part.

I'd purposely invited him and the girls to a bar that was closer to his place than mine or theirs. So, the four of us ended up crashing in his room for a while, laughing and cutting up. Finally, Alexi and Fiona, who were privy to my ruse, left, and I pretended to fall asleep on Gib's bed.

I closed my eyes and waited for him to climb into bed, so I could begin the drunken groping. He never showed up, though, and eventually I fell asleep for real.

Around two in the morning, I got up to pee and when I came back, I saw him lying on the floor next to the bed. Undeterred, I lay down next to him. I nuzzled into him, and slowly let my hand wander down to his more *sensitive* areas. Gib grabbed my hand before it landed on the happy spot, and propped me up next to his bed. Then, with his eyes locked on mine, he brought his big, beautiful hand up to cradle my face, and whispered, "I don't take advantage of people when they are drunk." Then, he lifted me up and laid me on his bed, covering me with blankets.

I never really appreciated the gentlemanly behavior thing, thinking it was a bunch of old-fashioned bullshit, but not anymore. Whether he knew I was playing him or not, the fact that Gib refused to act on my drunken flirtations cast the dye for me. He was forever to be my one and only.

NINE

GIB

I WAS BOTH HAPPY and concerned about having friends. On the one hand, it felt good no longer having to eat or study alone. I now had people to go out with, or better yet, hang out with. On the other hand, I was terrified things would turn out like they had with Chase and Olivia. Part of me just didn't trust friendships anymore, so I was constantly on the lookout for whatever my three new friends had to hide.

We were from vastly different backgrounds. While an air of wealth seemed to ooze from their pores, there was something sweet and down to earth about them as well.

Allen McCartney was by far the nosiest of the three.

"So, tell me about your family?" he asked, out of the blue one day.

"Um, well, I lived with my mom and her sister, as well as my siblings," I said, intentionally keeping things vague.

Of course, I immediately felt suspicious. Did he know about Olivia and Chase?

Then, he asked about my high school years, college, and what my friends were like. The man seemed to constantly pepper me with questions. That's when I realized he was just digging for information.

At first, I was nervous about revealing too much, afraid that learning I'd been a foster child until graduating from high school would drive them away. After a while, though, it became more about dodging his never-ending needling. It felt more like a game to keep information from him, than it was about not wanting to tell him.

Besides, Allen was one of the cutest men I'd ever met, and I enjoyed screwing around with him more than I probably should've. He'd pout when he didn't get his way, which always sent cold shivers down my spine, especially as I imagined what it would be like to take that cute bottom lip into my mouth, and bite it ever so lightly.

"God, I'm pathetic," I said to myself in the bathroom mirror, following a study session. Images of me kissing Allen swam through my mind, and well, I had more than a few visions of other things we could do together.

"He's a friend. He's a friend," I forced myself to recite to my reflection.

As much as I fantasized about Allen, or tried not to, I had actually grown closer to Alexi than to him or Fiona. We spent a lot of extra time together as study partners, and I confided in her more about my past. When she asked why I avoided telling Allen, I confessed it was just more fun to keep him guessing.

"So," Alexi said just as we were finishing a big assignment, "Why do you keep changing the subject when Allen asks personal questions?"

"Do I?" I asked, finally getting used to Alexi's directness, which if I was honest, sorta reminded me of Olivia.

"You know you do, now spill. What's going on?"

I laughed. "At first, his questions made me nervous, but now, I just like seeing his cute, pouty look, when he doesn't get what he wants."

Alexi watched me for a few minutes before she smiled. "You know, he's such a playboy, has been since he hit puberty. Most of the time, people give him anything he wants. I think you're good for him," she said, shaking her head.

I smiled. "He's a good guy, I think, but yeah, I'm mostly just screwing with him."

Alexi returned my smile. "I approve, and keep it up! But, Gib?" she asked, causing my smile to drop. "Don't keep yourself at arm's length. We all like you, and want to get to know you, okay?"

I nodded. "Yeah, I'll try not to be too much of a lone wolf."

"Good. Now, you've told me about yourself, so it's my turn to share something about me."

Alexi was a powerhouse of a woman, even Olivia and Miss Margaret would respect how she handled herself, but she blushed as she spoke, "You have to promise not to repeat this, though, okay?"

I nodded hesitantly, unsure where this was going. "I think I might be in love with Fiona," she said, biting her bottom lip. "But, I'm sure she only likes men. I just needed to tell someone that, and I couldn't tell Allen, because... well, because we're just too close."

I leaned over and let Alexi pull me into a hug, "Your secret is safe with me," I said. "But, maybe you should just tell her, you know, so you don't have to hold it in."

"Oh, God, no!" she yelled. "I would... no, it would be horrible, and put our friendship in jeopardy. Not worth it, our friendship is not worth losing over something as stupid as love."

I forced myself not to chuckle at her freakout. "Okay, well, it's our secret, no matter what you decide to do."

She nodded and left soon after. I thought about Olivia and Chase, and was immediately filled with the familiar sadness and longing I always felt when thinking of them. Alexi was right, of course. Why damage a true friendship over something as stupid as love?

Why had Olivia and Chase decided to put our friendship, our family, in jeopardy over their relationship? The resentment came roaring back, and hit me square in the gut, steeling my resolve not to return home for the holiday break. I couldn't stomach the idea of pretending to be the happy family we weren't anymore, so I made the excuse that I needed the time to study, and made other plans.

⤜⤏

Christmas night was fun as long as I was with people, which was how I ended up surrounded by Alexi's family at their humongous home. I thought the old Victorian I grew up in was a monster, but Alexi's parents' house was at least three times the size. My Southern, Protestant sensibilities kicked in, and I couldn't help but wonder why anyone would need, or for that matter, want that much space?

Even with Olivia, Chase, Miss Margaret, Mrs. Simmons, and me, the Victorian had felt too big. Of course, my opinion may have been skewed by the fact that cleaning it often fell to us kids. Even though Miss Margaret hired a maid service once a month for the deep cleaning, it seemed like my entire childhood could be described as Windex or Pledge eau de toilette.

While I'd made excuses not to spend the holidays with them, I missed Olivia and Chase like never before. I ended up calling them around midnight their time and Olivia answered. When she heard my voice, she burst into tears. "I was so scared you wouldn't call," she cried. I couldn't help but shed a few tears too, but I stifled it, not ready for them to know how emotional I was feeling.

Olivia put me on speakerphone, and she and Chase told me about spending the day with Miss Margaret. She was still living in the old Victorian, because Olivia and Chase had told her they couldn't afford the place until their trust money was available, and didn't have time for maintenance with their new baby and jobs anyway.

Mostly, I suspected they didn't want to displace Miss Margaret, though childhood memories lurking around every corner of that house probably factored into their decision too. I couldn't imagine living in the old mansion, with its constant reminders of the family I felt I'd lost. It was one of the reasons I avoided going home.

"Hey, I got a new internship with Mr. Patterson's law firm," Chase said, disrupting my wandering thoughts.

"Cool," I replied halfheartedly. "That way, you can decide if you like litigation or defense, since he does both."

Chase had decided to attend law school starting next fall. He didn't say it, but I knew he was waiting for access to the trust fund, so he wouldn't have to borrow money from Miss Margaret. Of course, that made me feel guilty for having accepted her offer to pay for medical school. I had no idea how much money Miss Margaret had or didn't have. I hoped to God I wasn't spending her retirement money. If I was, I'd simply pay her back using my trust fund. There was more than enough in it, and hopefully, I'd have plenty of money coming in after I graduated, or at least after completing my three-year residency.

Our conversation grew stilted the longer we were on the phone. Luckily, hearing their baby wailing in the background gave me the perfect excuse to cut the call short. I wondered if I would ever be able to ease the awkwardness between us. I really wanted to, but I didn't know how.

The next day, Allen, Alexi, Fiona, and I were heading out of town to go sledding on a hill they all liked. This winter had been particularly cold, and there was plenty of snow to play in. When Allen asked if I did much sledding growing up, in another attempt to get information out of me, I subtly looked at Alexi and winked.

"Allen," I said, "—you know it doesn't snow much in the South." Then, I grabbed Alexi's arm and pulled her toward the hill.

I thought of my sib... I meant, Olivia and Chase, all day while sledding with my new friends. The snow was so beautiful and thick here, nothing like the muddy snow in Tennessee. I yearned for them to be here, knowing they would have enjoyed the adventure as much as me, but they had an infant and other responsibilities now. We weren't carefree kids anymore.

I almost called them again that night, but decided to send an email instead.

Hey, went sledding today. You wouldn't believe how much snow there is here. Beats the heck out of the old barn hill, not that we didn't have some good sled runs there back in the day. I miss y'all, send me pictures of the baby.

It was hard for me to think of them as married with a baby. Of course, I'd been away at school during most of Olivia's pregnancy and had only spent about a week visiting home the summer after the baby was born. I'd elected to stay on campus over summer break and take a couple courses to get ahead of the curve. To be honest, I mostly wanted to avoid the discomfort of being home.

The holiday merriment continued with my new friends the following day. Allen baked cookies, while Alexi, Fiona and I sat on the couch in front of the cozy fireplace. I was not domestic, but I could hold my own in the kitchen if needed. Both Mrs. Simmons and Miss Margaret believed children should know how to take care of themselves, be they a boy or girl, so Olivia, Chase, and I all knew how to cook.

The smell of freshly baked cookies wafted through the living room as Allen passed them around, flirting with me like there was no tomorrow.

Alexi and Fiona confronted me the moment Allen disappeared back into the kitchen to plate some cookies for Alexi's parents. "So!" Alexi said.

"So, what?" I asked as I popped a still-warm cookie in my mouth.

"God, you are obtuse," Fiona grumbled.

"What?" I asked, confused.

"You know Allen likes you," Fiona said. "Why are you pushing him away?"

"Oh," I said, and looked to Alexi for some support. She gave me none. "I... well, you know I was a foster kid, right?" I'd finally confessed that to them over Thanksgiving, and hoped opening with that now would garner enough sympathy to keep them from diving too deep into my psyche. When they nodded, I said, "Well, I have two siblings... they're foster siblings, actually, and when they... um... when they got together..." I shook my head as I trailed off, at a loss for how to continue the awkward conversation, and I could tell by the looks on their faces that Alexi and Fiona understood.

"You're afraid you'll lose again?" Alexi asked. Just her acknowledging what I'd always felt—that I had lost my siblings—was enough to put me into an emotional tailspin. I didn't want to cry in front of them, so I kept my lips sealed and nodded.

After a moment, I managed to find my voice again. "It felt like a betrayal," I admitted. "I don't want to date Allen, *because* he's my friend. It would change our whole dynamic, and I don't want to ruin a good thing. It wouldn't be fair to you and Fiona for us to hook up." Alexi laughed over my use of the term hook up. "What?" I asked, smiling at her laughter, and grateful it helped ease my tension.

"You really aren't the hooking-up type."

"Ugh, I know," I agreed, and shook my head at the truth of that.

"Listen, no matter what does or doesn't happen with Allen, you're stuck with us. We're friends, and no amount of dating within our little group, or outside it, is going to change that. We're the Apple Fritter Gang, and we always will be."

I nodded, and said in all seriousness, "I don't want to jeopardize our friendships for a quickie. It's best to let friends be friends, and lovers be lovers."

Alexi and I both knew I was full of shit about my quickie comment, given our whole demisexual discussion months ago, but I spoke the truth about everything else. She looked at me with what could only be described as frustrated resignation, and I knew my words had struck a chord. She was thinking about her and Fiona, and all of the ways making a move on our possibly straight friend could go sideways. Sex and love could fuck up a situation. *Just look at me and my sib... I mean, look at Olivia, Chase, and me.*

TEN

ALLEN

I SAW HIM FROM across the bar, and immediately made my move. He was tall like Gib, but more muscular. *Why am I comparing every other man to the one I want, but can't have? How fucked up is that?*

The guy had noticed me too and met me halfway. "Hey, wanna get out of here?"

Direct, I thought. Oh well, why pretend I was here for anything else. If I'd been on Grindr, it would've been *wham bam, thank ya, Sam*. Why should a bar be any different?

I'd drunk too much and was feeling the effects. "Fuck it, why not?" I said, and tugged the man out of the bar. I intended to hail a taxi when he began pulling me toward what I assumed was his car.

Before I could get buckled in, he leaned over and began kissing me and nibbling my neck. I leaned my seat back as he slipped his hands into my pants.

"Oh, God. Yeah, Gib, that's amazing."

He froze, and it took my inebriated brain a moment to realize I'd called him Gib. No wonder, seeing as for the past few months, every time I jacked off, it was to the image of Gib's face.

"Sorry," I said, and the man, whose name I still didn't know, shrugged, and started to pull my underwear down.

"No, wait," I said. "I can't do this. I'm not gonna fuck you when I'm thinking of someone else."

The guy shrugged again. "Makes no difference to me. It's just a fuck."

"Yeah, I need to go," I said, then opened the door as I quickly zipped my pants back up. Sexcapade aborted. I flagged down a passing cab, and made a hasty retreat back to my place.

I arrived home feeling even more unsettled than in the wannabe hook-up's car, and called Fiona, telling her what happened.

"Allen, if your feelings for Gib are that strong, you need to tell him."

"Tell him what? That I've developed feelings for him, even though he's made it clear he's not interested? No, Fiona, I can't just tell him." Damn my voice for cracking on that last bit. So much for my playboy reputation.

Fiona ended up coming over and consoling me, since I couldn't seem to stop my tears. I had it bad for Gib Ridley, and nothing was going to make it better.

Eleven

GIB

ALLEN HAD BEEN MORE distant toward me in the months after Christmas, not that I could blame him. I had put up a pretty cold shoulder to rebuff his flirting, and made clear I wasn't going to let anything more than friendship develop between us. As it was, though, our friendship felt strained.

With the school year ending and needing a break, I decided to go home for the summer, and took an internship at old Dr. Wilson's clinic.

Returning home also meant seeing my family. I was determined to patch things up with Olivia and Chase, and our relationship did improve over the first few weeks, well... until they made their next announcement.

"We're pregnant, again!" Olivia announced one night as I worked the barbeque. I looked up to see Chase looking at me, and I forced a tight smile, which apparently came across more like a grimace. When I turned to Miss Margaret, I saw the same look of disappointment.

At first, I thought it might be from Olivia and Chase's announcement, but then I realized she was upset at my reaction. It was no secret I hadn't done a good job of accepting Olivia and Chase's relationship from the start. Clearly, despite my best efforts, I was still struggling with it.

I left the party soon after we ate, telling them I needed to get some rest before having to work the next day. Of course, since it was only six in the evening, I knew I wasn't fooling any of them.

I was being petty, but I was only just coming to terms with their being married with one child. Being blindsided with the news of them expecting another baby was more than I could handle. Not that I didn't love my niece Chrissy, or was happy for her that she'd soon have a little brother or sister. I, of all people, knew what a difference having siblings had made growing up.

The next night, Miss Margaret, who I was staying with, chastised me. "Gibbon." She always used my full name, and her clipped tone had me feeling like a scolded child all over again. "I know you are struggling with Olivia and Chase. Honestly, I did too at first, but there really isn't anything wrong with them being together."

She stopped before she said what I knew was on her lips. *You aren't really related.* That was the sticking point, but family wasn't limited to sharing genes or the same last name. We'd been raised together, side by side and in this very house, by the same two no-nonsense

Southern women who'd cared for us like their own. To me, we were family.

I sat down on the formal settee with my head in my hands. I knew not to get emotional with Miss Margaret, so I tried to keep clear of that. "Miss Margaret... Chase, Olivia, and you are all the family I've got. They are... *were* my siblings. The fact that everyone just throws their hands up saying we're not actually related, so I shouldn't have a problem with it, is the thing that hurts me most."

I stopped talking and looked out the open front door at the expansive lawn, my mind spinning with the admission. I hadn't said that to anyone else. In a surprising move, Miss Margaret came over and sat next to me.

She put her hand over mine, and said, "Let me share a story that might help you avoid the same mistake I made. When Ruby married Charles, I was jealous. Not of their relationship, but that someone besides me had become an important part of Ruby's life. You see, when we were young, our father was, well, cold and strict, so Ruby and I only had each other for support. When she fell in love with Charles, I felt like I'd lost my sister, and I let my jealousy keep us apart for years. It wasn't until I moved in with you all after Ruby got sick that it changed."

She looked at me and patted my hand, although making the comforting gesture was clearly difficult for her. "I lost crucial years with my sister, because I allowed my own jealousy to keep us apart. I see you doing the same thing with Olivia and Chase, and it's hurting all three of you. You may not be feeling jealous, but you do feel something... Maybe betrayed."

Miss Margaret looked away, clearly trying to keep from crying, which made my own throat tighten. When she turned back, she looked me straight in the eye. "Don't wait until they are sick or worse, gone, before you get past the stuff holding you back. It's one of my biggest regrets, and made losing Ruby so young harder to bear."

Miss Margaret got up and walked out of the room. I heard the powder room door open and shut, and knew she'd gone in there to cry. I needed some fresh air to clear my head and decided it was a good time to take a walk around town. Miss Margaret was right, I needed to forgive Olivia and Chase before I ended up regretting everything, but it was up to me alone to figure out how to do that.

I called Olivia and Chase the next day and asked if we could meet that evening. Miss Margaret had agreed to babysit Chrissy. She'd readily volunteered after I explained my plan to come clean to them, then hugged me and said how proud she was of me for making amends. Seriously, I had no idea who Miss Margaret was any longer, but I liked the change. She'd softened considerably since Mrs. Simmons's death and no longer resembled the drill sergeant who'd raised us.

The three of us met at our favorite pizza place in the town square, despite my not feeling like eating. I had the same sick feeling in the pit of my stomach that happened any time we discussed their relationship. It was becoming a familiar feeling.

Olivia and Chase were clearly as nervous as me. It had been a long time since I'd called a family meeting, and seeing as I'd been largely avoiding them both for the past two years, they probably weren't sure what to expect.

I wasn't prepared to jump into the conversation, so I bided my time while we all ordered pizza. After placing our orders, we settled at a quiet corner table, and I finally felt ready to talk. Olivia and Chase both looked at me expectantly.

I didn't try to quash my emotions, not this time. If I was going to find my way through this, I'd have to let them see how I felt. "I've been *so* fucking pissed at you two since Mrs. Simmons died. Last night, Miss Margaret had a 'come to Jesus' talk with me about how much time she lost with her sister, because of jealousy, and convinced me to try to make this right between us."

Silent tears were running down Olivia's face, but I couldn't stop to try and make my words hurt less. If we were going to reconcile this, I needed to have my say.

"We were a family. Like blood, but not..." I paused, trying to find the right words. "When the two of you started dating and then got married, for God's sake, you changed that. Now I have to endure the *well, they aren't really related* comments all the time when people try to justify how it's okay for you to be together. The problem is, I always considered us related, but now, I can't. I've spent the past few years retraining myself to stop calling you my siblings. I still slip up sometimes, and it hurts every time."

I'd run out of words, and I felt wrung out. There was so much anger and hurt wrapped up in everything I'd said, I just hoped my message got across, because I didn't have it in me to attempt a repeat.

The three of us sat in silence, them apparently waiting for me to continue, and me struggling with what else to say. We all avoided eye contact as the minutes ticked by waiting for our food, the mood heavy and awkward as hell between us.

The pizza finally came, giving us a momentary reprieve. We shuffled the pizzas around, because the servers never gave us the right ones. Then Olivia looked me in the eye and said, "You *are* our brother. You always will be our brother. Our being together doesn't change that."

The anger rushed back, and I couldn't quash it any longer. "No, Olivia, it has changed. The world sees it differently, and it's changed how I see it. I'm not your brother, we aren't related."

I suddenly felt like I was going to suffocate. I put my napkin down and stood up. "I just need a moment," I told them as I walked out the door, and down the street to a bench in front of the old drug store.

I must have sat on the bench too long, because Chase and Olivia, carrying our boxed pizzas, eventually joined me.

"Come on," they both said at the same time, each holding out a hand to hoist me up. "We're going to the old barn hill. This requires more privacy than we have here."

I looked at them uneasily, concerned about revisiting one of our old haunts. "I heard the property got bought by a new family."

The two of them looked at each other, and smiled. "Yeah, it did. We're the new family. We used some of the trust money to purchase it. We're going to have a house built there one day."

I couldn't help but smile. As angry as I was at them, I knew how much we all loved the old barn hill, and the hours we spent hanging out there could easily define our childhood. "For real, you're not joking? You own the old barn hill?" Olivia just laughed and Chase beamed with pride. For a moment, we were back to being our old selves.

"Okay," I said, grabbing the top pizza box. "I bet I can beat you there. Old married people are slow and sad!" I exclaimed as I rushed up the road. Of course, I was no match for Chase and never had been. He outran me by at least a block and Olivia was pregnant, so she didn't even try to run, but laughed at me for being such a slow old man. Nothing new, she'd called me that since we were teenagers.

When we got to the old barn's foundation, we sat in our same old spots and began eating pizza. I finished mine first, which was also pretty much the way it always was, and lay back. "I totally hate you two," I said without any heat. My words were harsh, but we'd said it to each other so many times over the years that it'd become a term of endearment.

As they continued eating, I stretched out and stared up at the night sky. "You have every right to," Chase said. "We handled this all wrong. I guess we just took you for granted, and didn't think about the impact our relationship would have on you."

"'Cause, you both suck monkeys," I replied.

Olivia snickered. "You aren't ever going to grow up, are you?"

"No, probably not," I agreed. "I guess I have some pretty big news I've kept from you too." I sat up, so I could look them in the eye. "After I tell you, you have absolutely no right to do anything but say you're happy for me, got it?" I knew I was being an ass, but I wanted them both to feel what it was like to have personal shit dumped on them out of the blue. Yeah, I was a typical brother. "I'm gay. You're never going to have nieces and nephews." I stared at them, daring them to say anything. Instead, Olivia and Chase looked at each other, and I'd be damned if they didn't snicker. "What the fuck!" I shouted and got up to leave, seething. *They think this is a joke?*

"Stop, you dufus," Olivia said. "That is your *slap us in the face* information? Don't you know we already knew that?"

"Hell—" Chase chimed in, "—you almost drooled every time you caught a glimpse of Robert Poole all through high school. I could've sworn you even planned your class schedule around his for that very reason."

I didn't know whether to be annoyed or relieved that my big revelation hadn't even caused a blip on their radar. Of course, they knew, but I was still pissed I hadn't had that same insight about them. "So, you knew I was gay, but I didn't know you two were a-a thing?"

Olivia looked down, and Chase looked me in the eye. "Do you want to know why you didn't know?"

"Yeah, that might help!" I all but yelled.

"Before we both came to the Simmons' house, we'd already been placed together in another foster home. We were both still little, but we decided then we'd someday get married. When we came to live with Mr. and Mrs. Simmons, you became our brother, and we all but forgot about our promise." Chase looked off in the distance and waited a few moments, before continuing, "When we got to college, Olivia started dating that idiot. Do you remember him?" I moaned because both Chase and I hated him. Olivia just rolled her eyes at us. She knew how we felt about him, even though we never told her.

"When I saw her dating another guy, everything came back for me. I was livid. I was supposed to marry Olivia. I had always planned to marry her. She was the only woman I ever intended to marry. Seeing her with that... that..."

"Piece of shit," I added.

"Yeah, that piece of shit," Chase agreed. "Something inside me broke. I confronted her one night, and she cried and threw herself in my arms. That was the first night we were together."

"Oh, God, shut up!" I exclaimed. "I don't need all the details."

"I didn't give you any details, you schmuck," Chase said, but he was laughing. "It's always been Olivia for me. You were our brother, so things got confusing, but we were more..." Chase looked away again before adding, "We were always more."

Olivia reached over, tears streaming down her face again. "Chase and I didn't want to hurt you. When I told you, I didn't think you would even flinch. I was wrong to do that to you. I knew it when you threw up in the bathroom. I just didn't know how to fix it."

Chase took up the conversation. "We also thought the baby would make it better. You love babies and we just assumed that telling you we were expecting might smooth over our engagement news, but we obviously didn't think that through either."

Olivia's face was still downcast, when she added, "The look on your face that day broke my heart. I was so angry with you for not understanding, and I was angry at us for not doing a better job explaining how we felt about each other." She looked at Chase, then at me. "We both hoped the wedding and the baby would bring you back to us, but it all just seemed to push you further away."

The three of us sat in silence then, not knowing what to say next. Finally, I felt the ice around my heart begin to crack. I wasn't ready to forgive and forget, but I was ready to move on. I knew if I didn't mend the rift between us, a part of me would always remain broken and full of regret, just as Miss Margaret warned.

"This still hurts, I'm not going to pretend it doesn't," I said. "I needed you to be my siblings, and your relationship changed things, but I need you in my life whether as brother and sister, or my best friends. Either way, I *need* you."

Olivia came over, and in a rare show of affection between us, wrapped her arms around me. Chase followed shortly after, both of them holding me in a vice-like bear hug. The gesture warmed my slowly healing heart even more, and was exactly what I needed.

"We should tell you something," Olivia said, after we pulled out of the hug that left us all a watery, snotty mess. "You know Chase has been interning at the law office while getting his law degree?" I nodded. "Well, he's seen so many kids who've been bounced around between family members after a parent dies that we decided to have our wills drawn up."

My heart stopped, then restarted, only to start breaking again. I'd just got these two back in my life, and I couldn't imagine losing them, not again. I almost interrupted Olivia, but something in her expression caused me to remain silent.

"If anything ever happens to us, we want you to be the guardian of our children." For a moment, I couldn't breathe, trying to grasp what it would be like to lose them for real. I finally shook it off. Writing their wills didn't mean anything bad would actually happen, or that I'd ever be raising their kids. They were young and healthy, and just behaving like responsible parents.

With that reassurance in mind, I focused on the two people I loved most in the world. Just the thought of losing them sealed the fissure created by their relationship.

We were still a family, albeit a changed one, and I wasn't going to take that for granted ever again. I wouldn't become like Miss Margaret, lamenting the loss of her time with her sister.

"Okay, yeah," I managed to croak out. "I-I will, but damn you, you better never die, at least not before I do. I go first and I plan to live until my late eighties, at least. Got it?" They both laughed, and just like that, the heavy mood lightened. Not all our wounds had been healed, but the biggest were mended enough that we felt like a team again.

Spending the rest of the summer finishing my internship, and creating happy memories with Olivia, Chase, baby Chrissy, and Miss Margaret left me feeling surprisingly refreshed when I returned to Harvard that fall. Good thing too, since my third year of medical school was proving to be the worst thus far.

From the moment classes began, I felt like I was drowning. It was like being tied to a desk, chained to the bottom of a giant tank as it slowly filled with water... it was agonizing, overwhelming, and there was no means of escape. Pretty much any time I wasn't in class or sleeping, I was studying, just to keep my head above water. I knew if it hadn't been for my friendship with the Apple Fritter Gang, I'd have died under the pressure. Alexi especially kept the four of us studying like we needed to.

Despite my busy schedule, I made a point to text Chase and Olivia several times a day. Usually, I complained about all the studying, or questioned why I thought Harvard was a good idea. In turn, they reassured me I belonged here and was on my way to becoming a terrific doctor. Having them in my corner helped me push through my recurring doubts.

Chase texted pictures of Olivia and her growing baby bump, behind her back, of course. I teased her about how big she was getting, which she took in stride, but still gave Chase shit in our group text for snapping pictures without her knowing. Of course, later we learned why she was already so big... she was expecting twins.

I began to worry how they were going to handle two jobs and Chase attending law school, on top of caring for two infants and a toddler. I texted one day shortly after learning about the twins.

Me: *Y'all are fucked. How are you going to do all that?*

Olivia: *Their uncle is going to come home and help!*

Me: *LOL. You're confident of that are you?*

Olivia: *Yeah. You'll agree, or this very big, hormonal sister will come murder you in the night.*

Me: *I believe you.*

Med school continued kicking my ass, but I slogged through it, class by class and month by month. My academic advisor recommended that I do another internship to appear more desirable to a residency program, but I couldn't imagine not going home over the summer break to help Chase and Olivia.

I'd just have to find an internship close to home. I needed to have experience working in a larger clinical setting, much bigger than where I interned last summer. I had decided to go into family medicine, although it paid less than other fields, but I knew I wanted to work with patients of all ages.

Needing all the help I could get, I texted Chase and Olivia.

Me: *If you want this free babysitter to come home, you better start helping me find a decent size clinic to intern at this summer.*

Olivia had gone into business and worked for a consulting firm in Jackson, the largest town near them. She texted me back in less than a minute.

Olivia: *I know just the place, they have over 10,000 patients from five counties. My boss works with them, so I'll see if he can put in a good word for you. I'm sure when they hear you're a Harvard boy, there won't be any problems.*

Me: *You like to throw that around, don't you?*

Olivia: *Hell, yeah. I get all the credit for having a brother at Harvard, and don't have to do any of the coursework. It's a win, win!*

The word I wrote back rhymed with witch.

As I resumed studying, my mind kept going back to how easily we'd fallen into calling each other brother and sister again. It felt right, and I guessed I understood how even though I'd become their brother, Olivia and Chase never saw each other as siblings. That's not to say it wasn't still confusing as hell sometimes, but I was just grateful we were in each other's lives. For the first time in years, I was looking forward to spending summer at home.

Twelve

Allen

"THIRD YEAR SUCKS!" I yelled across my room, resisting the desire to start throwing things out of frustration. Instead, I sent a four-way text to Alexi, Gib, and Fiona.

Me: *Remind me again why I signed up to be a doctor? I hate studying. I should have ignored my dad and become a tennis coach.*

Alexi: *Because ball-handling skills aside, you're terrible at tennis.*

Me: *But just think, I could be outside parading around a tennis court in short shorts right now, instead of glued to my desk chair staring at these horrible books.*

Alexi: *Bitch, stop whining and get it done.*

Annoyed I didn't get sympathy from my friends, I texted Gib in a separate thread, and asked if he was ready for the quiz. He wasted no time texting back.

Gib: *NO!*

Me: *Me neither. But I don't have the brainpower to study any longer. Wanna blow this off with me... or blow something else?*

Gib: *You are a perv.*

Me: *So, is that a maybe?*

Gib never took the bait, even though I wished he would. I'd only become more attracted to him since trying to seduce him with my failed fake-drunk charade. He still took my flirting in stride and was as kind as ever, unlike the jackasses I usually seemed to attract.

A few minutes later, Gib's name popped up on my phone as it rang. "Do you need a study partner? You know you can't blow this off, right?"

"I know," I lamented. "I hate medical school!"

"Yeah, yeah, you've said that before, but you've got better grades than any of us." However true the assessment, I silently preened under Gib's compliment. *Damn, I'm pathetic.*

"That's because my dad has shoved this crap down my throat since I was a toddler."

"Stop," he said. "I don't want to hear your pervert remarks about shoving things down your throat."

I laughed out loud, because he really had read my mind. "You know me too well. Are you sure you won't marry me?"

"No, you're a slut. I only marry whores."

It had become an ongoing joke. I occasionally told him I'd charge him if it would make a difference, and he'd just laugh, saying I clearly didn't need the money.

"Hey, if the offer is for real, I could use a study partner," I said. "I'm sure if I don't have someone tie me down, I'm just going to end up at the bar getting drunk."

"I'm not going anywhere near bondage jokes with you, but okay. I'll text Alexi and Fiona and tell them we need an intervention. Besides, I always do better on our tests when we study together."

"Yeah, it seems to help. See you in an hour?"

"Yep," he said, and hung up.

Gib was careful not to be alone with me for too long. Always including Alexi and Fiona had become his way of keeping a buffer between us. Even though I loved them like sisters, I cursed them for being such effective cockblockers. Lately, it felt like Gib might be warming to the idea of us being more than friends, but I'd be damned if I knew how to tease that part out of him.

I hadn't made any moves on Gib since my botched drunk act, in which I'd infamously succeeded in getting into his bed, but not his pants. I'd spoken to Alexi about my dilemma shortly after that, and she told me he was concerned about losing our friendship. Of course, that made sense in my head, but not anywhere else in my body.

Gib was so fucking hot. Sometimes when we were sitting together studying, I'd catch a whiff of him—a strong masculine scent mixed with the citrussy soap he used—and be so turned on, I was afraid of embarrassing myself in front of the girls. I was also pretty sure Gib wouldn't appreciate my hard-on attempting a hands-on anatomy lesson with him during our study sessions.

I'd tried a few tactics to keep my true feelings hidden from Gib, including putting some distance between us, but between studying together and our four-way Apple Fritter Gang friendship, I couldn't keep it up for long. Unfortunately, the more I was around him and the deeper our friendship grew, the more I wanted him. Other than using the occasional half-joking innuendo as a means of release, it was becoming more and more difficult to push those feelings down. Since the unfortunate bar hook-up incident, where I'd called out Gib's name to a stranger giving me a parking-lot hand job, I'd lost all interest in other men. God, I still couldn't believe I'd been on a dry spell that long.

While Gib had called me a slut in jest, it had once been a totally appropriate label. I liked sex, I liked playing around, and I'd done both with my fair share of men throughout college. I was no prude, but for all my experimenting, I could now confirm I preferred things one-on-one. Clearly, I was a romantic queen at heart for all the good it did. Too bad Gib didn't see that in me.

The Apple Fritter Gang gathered with namesake pastries in tow for a hellacious study session, and fought our way through mountains of material to prepare for the quiz. I ended up sitting between Alexi and Fiona to keep myself from leaning against Gib. Between touching or sniffing him, I couldn't afford the distraction of sitting next to the man. I was lucky the four of us were great study partners, though, and the following day's quiz was a breeze.

Honestly, if it wasn't for those three, I would've probably dropped out of med school. It wasn't that I didn't love the art of medicine, but studying it was really not my thing.

Alexi, the most driven among us, had decided to become a surgeon. Fiona was going into plastic surgery. Gib was the heart of our group, and just wanted to make the world a better place.

I had decided to pursue pediatrics, but already knew I'd eventually go into administration. I figured I'd end up running a hospital. The world of business would be much more fascinating than dealing with the day in, day out of patient care.

I was scheduled to do my internship that summer at my dad's hospital in Queens, New York. I'd convinced him to pull Alexi into the same internship, and that if he knew what was good for him, he'd try to secure her residency as well. He already knew Alexi, because our families had been friends since she and I were in kindergarten, and anyone with eyes could see her remarkable work ethic.

I tried to convince Gib and Fiona to join us, but Fiona had already accepted an internship at a posh practice in Manhattan, and Gib told me he was headed home to Tennessee to be closer to his family. His sister was expecting twins near the end of the semester, and he wanted to be there to help out.

At the prospect of not seeing him for months on end, I almost decided to chuck my dad's internship and follow Gib to Tennessee. I even found the gumption to broach the subject as we sat together in the local pub, celebrating having survived that dreadful quiz.

"Hey, so I think I've had my fill of the East Coast for a while. I need a change of scenery, never been to Tennessee. How about we go together, and I'll do an internship with you."

"Ha, you're funny. You'd break the first week interning in my hometown."

"No, I wouldn't," I said, pouting. I tried to sound upbeat, even if his dismissal stung a bit.

He obviously didn't take my idea seriously, and I guessed it would be kind of stupid to trade interning at a big urban hospital with its forty new medical and surgical beds for a rural hospital that barely had forty beds total. Not seeing his handsome face and sweet smile every day was going to make for a long summer as we went our separate ways.

What the Apple Fritter Gang lacked in face time that summer, we made up for with our phones. I texted the three of them constantly, even though Alexi and I spent a lot of time together anyway. Our internships kept all of us busy, and as the summer wore on, it became clear I was never going to work in my dad's hospital again.

"Why haven't you completed your rounds yet?" my father asked me for the third time.

"Dad," I said quietly, so as not to draw unwanted attention, "—it's impossible to do that and finish all the other work you gave me."

"You aren't trying hard enough, Allen," he said in a huff as he walked away.

"Same shit, different day," I said under my breath, barely managing to resist throwing the stupid bedpan in my hands across the ward. I should've known the ridiculously high standards he'd held through school would be nothing compared to what he expected of me while interning under him.

I'd never felt hatred toward my dad until that summer, so when the internship mercifully ended, I told him under no circumstances would I do my residency with him. I'd rather toss my medical career away than spend years on end enduring his criticism and disapproval. He was hurt, but I could tell he was also relieved. No matter how much either of us tried, we would never be able to work together.

Alexi, on the other hand, bloomed under my dad's supervision. The two of them got along like champions. Although he had similarly high expectations of her, they weren't quite as unrealistic, and she seemed to enjoy meeting and exceeding them.

By the end of summer, I'd stopped texting the group about how much I wanted to murder my father and toss his body in the Hudson. Instead, I sent those messages just to Gib. I didn't want to risk sharing my sentiments with Alexi, who wore rose-colored glasses when it came to my brilliant surgeon father. I also liked that Gib and I had something just to ourselves. It might have been silly to think that way, but it helped get me through the tough final weeks.

Gib didn't talk much about his internship or anything personal, unless it revolved around his three nieces. I'd swear I had never seen so many baby pictures in my life. The guy was obviously gaga over the newborn twin girls and their two-year-old sister, who apparently clung to Gib like a baby chimp to its mother.

I must admit, seeing how much Gib loved his nieces warmed my heart. He'd be an amazing dad someday, which had me imagining what it'd be like to have kids with him, not that I was cut out for parenthood.

When my academic advisor had suggested I consider pediatrics, it wasn't because I loved and wanted to help kids, though I did. It was due to my ability to medically evaluate and treat young patients from a clinical perspective without getting too emotionally involved. I wasn't emotionally removed from the work, but I didn't wear my heart on my sleeve either. I never had... at least, not until meeting Gib. Whatever he wanted—babies, marriage, a house in Tennessee—I could see myself wanting, simply because I wanted him. I had it bad, and I couldn't deny my feelings any longer. If only I had the courage to tell him.

THIRTEEN

GIB

THE TWINS WERE BORN April third, and I had my last final of the school year on May first. Those final four weeks of classes between their birth and being set free for summer break were especially brutal, or maybe it just felt that way, because I was eager to get home.

The summer I spent with my family was one of the best of my life. I fell head over heels in love with my three nieces. Chrissy was totally undone by the arrival of her twin sisters, and clung to me for hours at a time. I became her pseudo-parent for the summer, seeing as Olivia and Chase had their hands full between work, school, and the babies. I'd never been around kids much, but helping care for Ruby and Margie, who were named after Mrs. Simmons and Miss Margaret, was a joy, even if it meant being on diaper duty.

Olivia's boss helped me secure an internship at a clinic in Jackson, and luckily, my work hours left me time to spend at home. If there was any doubt about how much I loved my eldest niece, I only needed to point to the number of torturous hours we spent watching her favorite TV show. Chrissy was obsessed with *The Wiggles*, an absolutely awful kids' show featuring grown men who danced around singing equally horrible songs.

"Dance, Uncle Gib, Dance!" she'd demand, and I'd comply every time, because Chrissy was already like a mini-Olivia, and I'd been trained for decades to obey that woman. I also adored my niece, and would do just about anything to make her smile and laugh, even when that meant dancing around the living room like a fool.

"Wiggle to the left, Wiggle to the right... Fruit Salad..." she sang gleefully every day, over and over. Most of the lyrics made no sense, but I'd much rather dance with Chrissy and ignore the creepy show.

Olivia had been on maternity leave since the twins were born, and Chase had given up his internship at a local attorney's office to fast-track his law degree. Even then, he left early every day for classes and studied late most nights. I didn't know how he survived on so few hours of sleep, but Olivia and I tried to let him get as much as possible. Miss Margaret sometimes came over to take a day shift with the babies, and a couple teenagers were hired to babysit as well, which was the only way Olivia ever got any sleep. I began to worry about how they would manage after I returned to school. Miraculously, by the end of July, the babies began sleeping through most of the night, so I spent the last month of summer break helping everyone adjust to having one less pair of arms. Miss Margaret ended up coming through in the end by hiring a full-time nanny. The woman was in her mid-thirties, and had gone back to work when her own child started kindergarten. Between the new nanny and Miss Margaret, Olivia and Chase would have the extra time and support they needed after I left.

As I prepared to go back to Boston, I felt like my heart was going to rip in half. Chrissy didn't understand why I was leaving, and when I tried to explain, she turned those big, beautiful doe eyes on me and let the tears flow. I ended up buying her a tablet and teaching her terrible two-year-old self how to send me pictures. During those last few weeks, Olivia let her speak to me via Skype while I was at the clinic. By the time I left, Chrissy knew how to get in touch with her Uncle Gib any time she wanted.

My first month back at school was even harder than I imagined. The combination of my fourth-year course load and missing my family was torture. I got texts every evening of pictures Chrissy had drawn. Miss Margaret helped her photograph and send them. I thought those daily pictures were what got me through my homesickness. Sometimes Chrissy sent me photos of the babies, but I knew she still kind of hated them, which made me laugh. I knew Olivia like I knew myself, and it was clear Chrissy was a chip off that block. The twins were destined to have their lives dictated by their big sister, but for now, they were just lucky she'd decided to let them live.

Over the course of our final year, the Apple Fritter Gang became closer in some ways, and more distant in others. We rarely had the same classes, since most of our courses focused on our chosen area of specialty. I missed not seeing Allen, Alexi, and Fiona as much, and our schedules left very little time to just let our hair down. Despite that, we held study parties for the few classes we had in common, and tried to study together as often as possible.

Allen noticed my heartache and homesickness the moment we returned to campus, and he tried to be comforting. "Hey," he said, when I was feeling particularly blue after getting one of Chrissy's pictures. "You really miss them, don't you?"

I just nodded, too overwhelmed by all the emotions to speak. Allen surprised me by coming over and pulling me into a hug. Normally I wouldn't have let him, determined to keep my distance, but I needed that hug so much, so I let him pull me close as I rested my head on his shoulder.

More surprising was that nothing about it was sexual and he didn't flirt with me, he just let me be. To be honest, his kindness did more to soften my shell than any flirting he'd ever done. Allen seemed to have changed, and I welcomed it.

As the school year progressed, he and I spent more time without the girls. Thankfully, his incessant flirting continued to decrease.

Mostly, when we were together, he'd listen to me whine about missing my family, or we'd talk about his concerns regarding where to do his residency, or how different he was from his dad. Allen was more serious, and as a result, I shared more with him than I ever had with anyone else.

I felt myself growing closer to him than I ever thought I would. I still kept the friendship boundaries pretty well in place, but there were times I allowed myself to imagine what it would be like to hold him or kiss him.

Allen was shorter than me by several inches and had a much smaller build. None of us had time to get the exercise we needed, but his body was toned, nonetheless. Occasionally, we'd bump up against each other by accident, and I could feel his warmth beneath his clothing. If we weren't friends, I would've pursued him long ago, but his playboy reputation preceded him, and I knew it would have been a short-term fling. I was glad I'd resisted over the years, but that didn't mean I couldn't think about him at night when I was by myself.

Despite the difficult classes and time spent studying, the school year flew by. The four of us came back together to study for the United States Medical Licensing Examination, and fortunately, we all passed step two. I applied to several residency programs in Tennessee. My residency was going to take three years, and I knew I wanted... *needed* to be as close as possible to my family.

I interviewed at several places, but none felt right, at least, not until I visited a non-profit health center that only accepted one resident at a time. The administrators were debating whether to keep their program open, but after meeting me and learning that I grew up just one county over, we both knew it was the perfect fit. Not only would I be making an impact in the community and the lives of patients that needed my care, but being near home meant having my family close and seeing my nieces grow up. I was excited for this next chapter in our lives.

Fourteen

Allen

I HAD NO IDEA what I was going to do for my residency program. After my painful internship last summer, I knew I couldn't work three years with my dad. Not to mention an additional three if I ended up going for another specialty, which I planned to do. In fact, I had a feeling if I was located anywhere near my father, he'd find some way to interfere. I was seriously thinking about applying somewhere on the West Coast, maybe Southern California? The thought of spending my off days on the beach sounded pretty awesome.

Of the four of us, I appeared to be the only one struggling to decide where to land after graduation. While I'd bet money on Gib setting his sights on Tennessee, he remained tight-lipped about his applications. Fiona, meanwhile, had already secured a residency at the Manhattan clinic she'd interned at last summer. I figured

Alexi's residency program choice was a foregone conclusion too.

"You won't believe it," Fiona said as she burst into my room one evening before the semester ended. "The upscale Manhattan clinic has offered me a residency!"

I laughed. "You so knew you were getting it. Did you get Alexi's text? She's in too." Fiona nodded, then stared at me. "What?" I asked.

"Where are you going to go, Gib? I mean, time isn't on your side."

I nodded, knowing there were a lot of graduates that didn't get a residency. It was an ongoing fear for anyone on the verge of graduating from medical school.

I shrugged. "I've applied at a few places, but..."

"But," she said. "Gib won't be there?"

I looked up, not even trying to deny it. "You too... I mean, Alexi, you and I... we've been together so long."

She came over and put her hand on my arm. "It'll be okay, Allen, but well..." She paused before taking a deep breath and letting it out slowly. "You really do have to move on this, promise me you will, okay?"

I nodded, and after she hugged me, she slipped out of my room to announce to the world she'd landed the perfect residency program.

I didn't tell Fiona, well, anyone, that knowing Gib would apply for residency close to home led me to apply for a position in Nashville. Honestly, I'd already considered the renowned hospital, but didn't give it too much thought since every medical school graduate in that part of the country would be applying there. More on a whim than thinking I stood a chance, I sent in my application. I heard back from a few hospitals in California first and even flew out to interview with one of them. Within moments of our meeting, I knew it was a bad fit. They wanted someone more like Alexi, a real go-getter who thrived on going above and beyond in everything she did.

I interviewed with a hospital in Florida next, and they offered me the position. I supposed I should've been relieved to have at least one offer, but something felt off about the place. It was owned by a giant corporation, and the prospect of rising through the ranks would be ideal for many, but was that the direction I wanted my career to take? I put them on hold for thirty days while I considered my other options, although there weren't many.

The Florida deadline was fast approaching when I got a call from Nashville. Impressed by my transcripts and internship, the board requested I fly out that week for an interview. I didn't want to jinx my chances, let alone alert Gib to my motivations, so I flew to Tennessee without telling anyone other than the professors whose classes I'd be missing.

I arrived in Nashville around six in the morning, with nine hours to spare until my interview, so I decided to do some sightseeing, and get a feel for the city I might be calling home for the next several years. Luckily, my Uber driver agreed to play tour guide, and I reserved him for the better part of the day.

Of course, we took in the tourist hot spots, including the Grand Ole Opry and Bluebird Café. Then some non-touristy parts of the city.

We ate lunch at Fat Moe's, where I had the greasiest, most delicious hamburger I'd ever tasted. By the time my driver dropped me off at the hospital a couple hours before my interview, I felt like I'd made a new friend.

I'd already arranged for a tour of the hospital before the interview, and was given a visitor's pass as one of this year's residents showed me around. Despite appearing harried, as one would expect of any first-year resident, she glowed when talking about working there.

As our tour continued, it became clear that this teaching hospital lacked some of the bells and whistles of newer medical facilities. This was a place that served the population and there was very little pomp and circumstance. Something about that raw honesty appealed to me, although I couldn't quite put my finger on why.

We then made our way to the conference room, where around twenty people had gathered for my interview. I hadn't been nervous about any of my residency interviews, at least not until all eyes were on me as I took a seat. I realized as I sat in my chair at the end of the long table that I wanted this position. I wanted it more than any other place I'd visited.

The realization dawned after the group had made their introductions, and before the rapid-fire questioning began. "Why don't you want to work at your father's hospital?" a younger member of the committee asked.

I hadn't really expected the question, not from here anyway. The other places I'd applied to told me they knew my father, by reputation if nothing else, and I figured it'd factored into my being invited to interview, but I had made a point not to disclose my family connection when applying to this hospital.

"I love and respect my father, as a man and a surgeon, but if I'm going to be the best physician possible, I need to make it on my own two feet," I replied, and it must've been a good enough answer, because I got more than a few nods of approval.

"It is our understanding that you have an offer from St. Augustine. If we made you an offer, do you know which hospital you would choose?"

I was taken aback for a moment, but managed to maintain my poker face. How could they possibly know about my other offer? The only thing I could figure was my dad must've gotten wind of my interview here and made some calls, not that he'd ever admit that to me.

Trying to hide my disgust that my father would pull strings even this far away, I smiled, and said, "Yes, I was impressed with St. Augustine, but I would prefer to do my residency here."

One of the older physicians raised his head to look at me for the first time. "Why would you choose Nashville over Florida?"

I was already flying by the seat of my pants with this line of questions, and it took me a moment to formulate an answer. "I arrived in Nashville for the first time this morning. I used the time to explore the city and get a feel for the community. I can easily envision myself living here. I also spent the past two hours touring this facility. To be honest, the other hospitals, including St. Augustine's, were newer with more modern equipment, but there's something different, something special about this place. You don't seem to serve only one segment of the population. You serve the wealthiest *and* the poorest, whoever needs care, and *that's* why I want to work here."

Honestly, that reasoning hadn't fully hit me until the words flew out of my mouth. For the first time ever, I'd spoken directly from my heart. My answer was met with a resounding silence, the face of the man who'd asked the question a blank canvas, so I didn't know whether I'd hit the mark or not.

Shortly after, I was asked to wait outside while the committee deliberated, which was unusual. Usually, decisions would take time, and notification of acceptance or rejection wouldn't come for at least a week. I got bored waiting and began texting everyone I knew, scrolling Instagram, and even playing some mindless game I didn't even know was on my phone. An hour later, people started filing out of the conference room.

I couldn't tell by their faces if the news was good or bad. Some smiled, but others wouldn't look at me as they passed. Finally, when almost everyone had gone, the woman who'd headed the meeting asked me to come back inside. The older physician who'd asked me why I'd chosen the hospital was still there, as was one of the current residents.

"We would like to offer our final residency position to you. Unfortunately, we will need your answer now. There are several other applicants, and with the end of the year being so close, we must let them know tomorrow whether we have already filled it or not."

Before I could even sit down, I replied, "Yes, of course, yes!" I could hardly contain my excitement. The older man smiled, but quickly looked down to stifle his expression.

The woman looked less enthused and just shook her head. I had a feeling it had been a vigorous debate, and that not everyone wanted me for the position, but it wasn't the first time I'd been in a tough spot. I would make Nashville work, even if it killed me.

The woman sighed, before saying, "I will send you the paperwork next week. Please, fill it out as soon as possible. I will also let Harvard know you have chosen us.

I nodded, and everyone stood up to leave as I waited to shake their hands. I was surprised when the older physician clapped me on the back, then as the other two exited the room, he winked at me, and said, "Us Harvard boys have to stick together," before heading out the door.

I realized at that moment he was the reason I'd been chosen, and it felt good having someone in my corner. I was happy and relieved to have found the right place for me, at least for the next few years. I wondered what Gib would have to say about my becoming a fellow Tennessean.

FIFTEEN

GIB

FINDING OUT THAT ALLEN had successfully applied for a residency in Nashville both shocked and excited me. I was slowly coming to terms with the fact that my East Coast friends would all be living miles away once I began my own residency in Tennessee. It hadn't occurred to me any of them would even consider applying anywhere in my home state. Sure, Nashville had a prestigious university and hospital, but they were notorious for selecting their own students as residents. Allen must have really made an impression to be accepted there.

I'd also admit I was a bit confused and maybe a little concerned about Allen's choice of location. I could think of at least a hundred facilities across the country more appropriate for his carefree spirit. When he'd told us he was interviewing in Florida and Southern California, we all three just nodded and assumed he would become Doctor Beach Bum.

I wasn't the only one shocked by Allen's decision. He waited until Alexi, Fiona, and I were all hanging out together to share his news. "So, I've accepted an offer for my residency."

"Florida?" Fiona asked.

He shook his head and looked over at me. "It's in Nashville."

All three of us just stared at him in silence for a few moments. I couldn't believe what I was hearing, and apparently, neither could they.

"What happened to Florida?" Alexi asked.

Allen smiled and shrugged. "Plans change."

When Alexi looked at me, then back at him, I got the impression I had a lot to do with his choice. Just the thought of that made my chest feel tight. Nashville had become cosmopolitan over the years, but it wasn't Boston, and it sure as hell would never be New York City. Had he decided to go all that way because of me? I was having a hard time breathing, and decided to sit down before the panic attack came on full force.

All three of my friends must've noticed, because Fiona changed the subject, but Allen had zeroed in on me. "What the hell is wrong with you?" he asked, sounding both concerned and a bit hurt.

I was still trying to draw in a full breath of air, as I croaked out, "W-why Nashville, Allen?"

"Because, it's an amazing opportunity to work with some of the national experts in my field."

"And?" I was still trying to catch my breath. "Is that the only reason?"

"No, of course not," he retorted, frustration pouring off him. "I wanted to escape the ever-present apron strings of my father."

I nodded, but wasn't satisfied. I really needed to ask if I was part of his decision.

Allen must've seen the question in my expression, because he blurted out, "And, yes, because I knew you'd be there, and I'd be in a strange place, but still have a friend close by. If I knew my being a hundred miles from where you grew up was going to freak you out, I wouldn't have applied."

Allen was pissed. In fact, I'd never seen him so angry. He stomped out of the room and disappeared down the hall. I'd finally gotten control of my breathing when I noticed both Alexi and Fiona were staring at me with disappointment written all over their faces.

"What?" I asked.

Fiona stood up and said in her matter-of-fact way, "You can be a total ass sometimes, Gib."

Alexi nodded in agreement. "Can't you see Allen is in love with you? Shit, he hasn't even been on a date with anyone for well, forever. You may not have the same feelings for him, but you could at least appreciate what he went through to be able to spend more time with you."

I just shook my head, not knowing what to say. I wasn't sure there was anything I could say. They were right, I'd been an asshole, and I had to fix it. "I'll go talk to him," I said.

"Damn right you will," Alexi said angrily.

I found Allen sitting outside my dorm on an old bench that looked like it had been there for hundreds of years. "Can I sit down?" I asked.

"It's a free country," he said, his shoulders slumped and his face stony. "And you go to school here too. Sit where you damned-well please."

I sat down and looked at him. "Do you have any idea why I was freaking out in there?"

"No fucking idea," he said, with as much venom as he could muster.

"Because I'm afraid you did all that for me." It was already a hard conversation for me, but I knew I had to be honest with him. I looked away and leaned back against the marble backrest. "You are someone who gives everything to those you care about. Over the past few years, we've grown really close. All four of us have. I also know you worry about me, I can see it when I'm talking about my family. Even though I've never really told you much, you know there are things I struggle with." I let that sit while I tried to form my next words. "You chose a fantastic hospital, but if you are moving there to take care of me, Allen, I can't stand the thought of that. You're so smart and gifted, you should go where you want, where you need to go."

Allen didn't look at me. Instead, he stared toward my dorm. "You make a lot of assumptions. Nashville is my first choice, because it has the whole package. I know when I leave there, I'll be a well-rounded pediatrician. I know the skills I learn there will be useful in many different areas of the medical profession. I did choose to apply there because I knew you'd be close, and that if I ever needed you, you'd be there for me." He looked over at me then, making full eye contact. "You are not, however, the reason I decided to accept their offer. I did that for me, for my career. Do I hope you'll be a part of my life while I'm there? Yes, I do. Why wouldn't I expect that after we've become this close? Do I expect you to coddle me and keep me from being lonely? Absolutely not."

Allen sighed, before continuing, "Gib, I'm leaving this area to get out from under my dad's control. Do you think I'd put myself in a situation where you could control my life? Damn you, Gib, I want to be my own man for a change. I'm fucking graduating from one of the most difficult medical programs in the world. Don't you think I'm smart enough to know where the hell I want to live and work for the foreseeable future?"

I could see the anger building back up, but I didn't know what else to say, so when he got up and left, I didn't try to stop him. Instead, I walked back to my room and faced the music with my other two friends. Luckily for me, they were more understanding this time, and tried to console me for being put in what felt like an impossible position.

The rest of the semester was torture, and not just because of my hellacious classes. Allen was ignoring me, and I felt his absence. I knew he felt betrayed and needed time to sort through his emotions, so I followed Alexi's advice to give him space. I had intimate knowledge of those emotions myself, and was beginning to understand what Olivia and Chase had endured when I'd given them the cold shoulder.

I managed to make it through finals without destroying my chances of graduating, though finals week left me feeling like my head had been in a vice. By graduation, I decided I'd given Allen enough space, so I started texting him again, telling him my family was coming up for the ceremony, and I was desperate for him to meet them. He didn't respond, and I was getting nervous that maybe I had destroyed our friendship after all.

The night my family arrived, though, Alexi and Fiona texted about meeting us at one of the restaurants in town. I was happy and surprised to see Allen with them. He smiled and shook everyone's hands as I introduced them and played with the babies, even holding one of the twins before passing her around. Chrissy latched onto me and held on the entire night. I was beginning to think I'd end up carrying her across the stage to collect my diploma, but her grip loosened as she eventually fell asleep, and curled up beside me on the bench seat.

Allen made conversation with everyone, and I could tell Miss Margaret really took a shine to him. The only problem was that Allen refused to even look at me. By the end of the night, I felt worse than I had when he was avoiding me altogether.

When we got up to leave, Allen grabbed the check. I tried to take it from him, but the look he gave me could refreeze the Arctic. So, supper was on Allen. When I looked over at Olivia, who'd watched the whole exchange, she was trying to stifle a smile. I gave her my own look, telling her to fuck off, but it just made her giggle out loud.

I walked everyone out while my friends—I still counted Allen among them—hugged my family, and told them how happy they were to finally meet.

The second we were back in their hotel room, Olivia looked at me, and asked, "So, what did you do?"

"What? Why do you assume I did something?" Even Miss Margaret laughed at my question.

"Honey," she said. "That boy was sweet on you, and you spurned him somehow."

I looked at Miss Margaret in shock. I'd never told her I was gay, so how would she know about Allen? Had Olivia or Chase said something to her? I was in the middle of giving them the angriest face I could summon, when Miss Margaret smiled at me. "You think I didn't already know? And, no, before you go after your siblings, they didn't tell me. Parents just know these things, honey. Besides, what is it they call it these days when you can tell? Gay radar or something like that?"

"Gaydar," Olivia said, clearly resisting the urge to laugh out loud. I just scowled at her again.

"Sweetheart, I was going to ask you," Miss Margaret said. "I wanted you to tell me yourself, but I guessed you never would. I honestly didn't mean to blurt it out like I did."

"Don't worry," I said, still glaring at my siblings. "Blurting out important stuff is what we do."

I gave Miss Margaret a big hug. "So, you're okay with it?" I asked.

"Well, I should be since I'm a lesbian."

All three of us froze and stared at Miss Margaret. "Come again?" Chase managed to ask.

A blush crept over Miss Margaret's cheeks, certainly a first time for that. "I just figured you already knew," she said. "I didn't mean to blurt that out either."

Olivia was the first to laugh, then Miss Margaret, followed by all of us. "No," Olivia managed to say. "No, we didn't know."

Chase then asked, "Are... are you seeing anyone?"

Miss Margaret blushed again. "Well, off and on. Nothing serious, though. Now enough about me," she fussed. "Aren't we here to give your brother a hard time?" Then, she looked at me, batting her eyes like a schoolgirl.

I shook my head, turned, and stuck my tongue out at my siblings. "Y'all wear me out," I said as I walked toward the door to leave. "All of us need a lesson on when to tell stuff, and when not to." That triggered another round of laughter from us all.

I loved having my family in the crowd at the graduation ceremony. Afterward, we all went out to dinner to celebrate. Chase and Olivia lasted until the kids began to crash. They took the kids and hailed a cab back to their hotel. The rest of us went to a local bar where there was music and a place to dance. Miss Margaret had really hit it off with Fiona's parents, and they sat in a corner laughing and gossiping. I could guess the subject included parts of my childhood, since occasionally they looked my way before chuckling about something.

I danced with Fiona and Alexi, while Allen actively avoided me. Finally, I'd had enough. I spotted him at the bar by the dance floor, and I went for him, grabbing and pulling him out the front door.

"Why the hell are you avoiding me?" I asked. He looked stunned for a moment. I doubted he considered I'd confront him, at least not in public.

It didn't take him long to regain his senses, though, and he tried to push past me back to the party. "No, I'm not letting you go back until you tell me what the hell has been going on." I could hear my own Southern drawl, which rarely happened except when I was really tired, drunk, or in this case, mad.

"You know damn well why I don't want to talk to you. You're a total jackass, Gib." I saw the tears and knew I'd pushed him to the brink. Allen looked utterly lost, and I couldn't help but draw him into my arms.

He resisted and fought me at first, but it didn't take long for him to melt into the hug. I felt the tears staining my shirt, and I ran my hand over his head, speaking quietly to him about it being okay.

Finally, he pulled away, but still didn't meet my eyes. "I know you don't feel the same way about me as I do about you," he said, still sniffing. "I'm not pathetic, Gib. I didn't... wouldn't go to Nashville just for unrequited love. I treasure our friendship, or at least I did, but if you think I'm just running around trying to win your affection, then I don't think we can be friends." The tears were streaming down his face now.

Maybe it was the wine, the moment, or his tears that propelled me, but I cupped the side of his face in my hand. "It isn't that I don't have the same feelings for you, it's that I'm afraid acting on them will destroy what we've got."

"That's almost worse," he said with another flash of anger, pulling his face from my hand. "You mean you've felt the same... feelings for me, but you haven't acted on them because you're afraid? Afraid I couldn't distinguish between you as a friend and you as a lover?"

"Not you, *me*." I looked at my feet, but kept talking, "When my foster brother and sister took their relationship to the next level, I felt betrayed. I almost threw away my family, because I couldn't separate our sibling relationship from their love for one another. It took me years to come to terms with it, and the pain still rises up from time to time to bite me in the butt." Then, I looked Allen in the eye and saw he was hanging on my every word.

"I do care about you, and I think about you... *that way* from time to time too, but if I can't manage my own family dynamics, what would happen when you get tired of me? Would I be able to continue to be your friend, or would I lose you?"

I sighed deeply, then pulled Allen to me again. "You don't understand what it's like to lose your family. I lost mine when I was about the same age as Chrissy. I remember going from one home to another and feeling terrified of the people. Some of them were mean, and others didn't even notice I was there. All that changed when I arrived at the home of Mr. and Mrs. Simmons. They were different from the start, and before I knew it, I felt they were family, like I belonged with them. When Olivia and Chase arrived a few months later, I was ecstatic about having my own brother and sister, and we loved each other from the moment we met."

Allen pulled back and took my hand. He led me over to a bench and we sat down together.

"We were only nine years old when Mr. Simmons died. Mrs. Simmons was diagnosed with MS a couple years later. All three of us thought we were going to lose her too. It changed us, made us wary of others. We even kept Miss Margaret at a distance after she took over caring for us. I don't think we realized that until recently, though. When Mrs. Simmons died, it crushed me. I found out the night we buried her that Olivia and Chase had started dating, and for me, it was like they announced they were done with me, like we weren't a family anymore, and I was alone in the world again. In many ways, I'm still that little boy who lost his parents. I'm too afraid to date you, Allen. I'm afraid I'll lose you."

It was my turn to cry. I had, at some point, laid my head on Allen's shoulder as I wept. I'd never told anyone my story. My fears were old and deep, but I knew if I didn't tell Allen the truth, I'd lose him for real.

I didn't know how long we sat there before Allen pulled me up, and guided me somewhere more private, so I could cry without publicly embarrassing myself. I was grateful for his thoughtfulness. The area was crawling with people since it was graduation, and seeing me crying like a baby on what should be a happy occasion would've drawn attention.

When I was finally out of tears, I realized I was lying down on a secluded bench with my head resting in Allen's lap. He was brushing my hair away from my face with such tenderness, and seeing the compassion and understanding in his face sealed my fate. At that moment, I felt a connection unlike anything I'd ever experienced, and I knew I was his.

I sat back up, faced him, and said, "Tell me what you want. I'll do whatever you want."

Allen leaned in to cup my face and kissed me. "I love you, and have for quite a while. I want you to let me love you, and for you to love me back." He never broke contact, stroking my cheek with his thumb as I nodded, and closed the space between us for another kiss. It started soft, but quickly turned heated as years of bottled emotions, want and need poured out of me. Fortunately, we were secluded by a hedge, because once I started kissing Allen, I wasn't sure I'd be able to stop, not until I'd tasted every part of him.

Allen pulled back at one point, and laughed. "Damn, I really thought you didn't like me."

"You were wrong," I all but growled.

He laughed even harder, and without warning, jumped up from the bench, and yelled, "Gib Ridley just kissed me!" I chuckled before getting up and kissing him again.

"I plan to do a whole lot more than that very soon."

The smile on Allen's face disappeared, and was re-placed with an expression of longing. "Don't promise me something you aren't willing to give," he warned, but with a hint of his old cheekiness that made me smirk.

"Oh, I plan on giving *and* taking... all night long!"

Sixteen

Allen

THE PROMISE ENDED UP being an empty one, at least for the moment, because Gib's siblings found us and dragged us all to a party on campus that our traitorous friends, Alexi and Fiona, told them about. It ended up being more fun than I anticipated. We danced, sang bad karaoke, and danced some more.

After Gib and I came clean to Alexi and Fiona, we met Chase and Olivia and drank until we were drunk. Well, Olivia couldn't, because she was still breastfeeding, and Gib ended up not drinking to keep her company. Alexi told me she'd also invited my half-brother, Lance, but he'd bowed out, which I'd expected, since he could barely stand me.

In the wee hours of the morning, Chase and Olivia caught a cab back to their hotel, while the rest of us all stumbled back to our dorm rooms, exhausted but happy.

Gib and I ended up sleeping together but because I was smashed, we just cuddled. But, oh my god in heaven, even still wearing clothes, feeling his warm body pressed up against mine with his armed wrapped around me all night long was the most amazing thing to ever happen to me.

The next morning came too early, and I avoided getting up when Gib went to meet his family for breakfast.

After a few more hours sleep, my phone rang. Of course, I ignored it, just like I was trying to ignore the ringing in my head. When the fourth round of shrill rings echoed through the room, I answered, "What?"

"Don't speak to your mother that way," Mom said, and I groaned.

"Mom, you know I was out late last night..."

"Regardless, this is the day after your graduation. It's *my* time today."

I'd spent the entire day yesterday with my father, stepmother Kassidy, and grumpy half-brother Lance, who would've clearly rather been anywhere but with us.

"Okay, Mom," I said, not wanting another lecture about how I needed to share time with both my parents. "Give me a few minutes and I'll meet you. Want to get brunch?"

"Yes," she said curtly, then told me to call her when I was up and dressed.

I moaned and forced myself into the shower. It wasn't that I had a hangover as much as I was still coming down from studying for months on end. My body was automatically shutting down now the stress-induced adrenalin was no longer coursing through me.

I quickly texted Fiona and Alexi on our group thread. The women texted back telling me they couldn't join Mom and me, because they had plans with their own families. Gib texted to tell me his family were going to eat brunch at our favorite breakfast place.

Gib: *We haven't been able to get out of the hotel room yet, because the little ones have been unhappy with their accommodations.*

I could hear the humor in his text. From my studies, I knew kids, in general, didn't like change, and babies were far less likely to be amused by it.

I quickly texted Mom and asked if she minded joining Gib's family, and she texted right back, saying as long as it was with me, she didn't care where we ate or with whom.

I smiled. My mother was a handful, to say the least. She and my father despised each other, but she never disparaged him in front of me, which I appreciated. However, she made it clear she didn't want to see or spend time with him either.

As uncompromising as she was with my dad, that's how accommodating she was toward other people in my life. I assumed it was because of the years she spent working her family's hospitality business.

I jumped into the shower and got dressed, only to find a waiting text from Gib telling me his family was heading to the restaurant. "Dang, that was five minutes ago," I said out loud to my empty room.

I quickly texted Mom to meet me at the restaurant, brushed my teeth, and threw on shoes before rushing out the door.

Me: *Gib, my mom's coming with me, hope that's okay.*

Gib and his family had already arrived when I got there. I quickly dashed in and greeted Chase and Olivia, who looked as exhausted as I felt. Their foster mom sat regally at the end of the table, while all three of the other adults, including Gib, were dealing with the little ones.

Despite that, Gib glanced up at me and winked, making me feel welcome.

They must've anticipated Mom coming, because when she arrived, she sat between me and Miss Margaret, and the two immediately hit it off and had tons to talk about.

Meanwhile, I was instantly adopted by Gib's niece Chrissy, an incredibly needy toddler who crawled into my lap and just sat there sucking her thumb.

Olivia chuckled. "That says a lot about you, because our strong-minded toddler doesn't usually have any patience for strangers. She seems to really like you, though."

Chrissy never left my lap the entire time we were at the restaurant. I'd barely managed to eat my own breakfast, and if it hadn't been for Gib moving his chair next to mine, so Chrissy could sit between us, I probably would've gone hungry.

Gib kissed me before he left with his family, assuring me he'd see me later. "I want to spend as much time with my family before they fly back home," he said, and before I could respond, Chrissy grabbed his hand and pulled him out of the restaurant.

I ended up going back to Mom's hotel with her, so we could also spend some quality time together.

Mom had raised me, and there was no way I'd have made it this far without her love and encouragement. Dad had argued with me my whole life, but Mom was the one I could lean on when I needed support. That was especially true when handling issues relating to Dad having unrealistic expectations of me.

I ended up going with her to a big gala the school was holding for graduates that evening. I was surprised to see Gib there, standing next to Alexi and Fiona.

Mom walked over with me, shook hands with Gib, and hugged Fiona and Alexi. "It's been awhile, girls. Are your parents here tonight?"

Fiona nodded and pointed at her politician father and mother, who were making the rounds among wealthy constituents. "Always campaigning," she said, and shrugged.

Alexi said her parents had to get back to work the following day, so they'd left earlier.

Mom smiled at Gib, and said, "I truly did enjoy meeting your family today. Your foster mom is quite the woman.

Gib looked confused and Mom turned to the girls to explain. "Margaret Latham was the owner and president of a small Memphis-based software company. I remember reading about her back in the nineties. Of course, she sold the company, but her software innovation has been used to enhance all the musical software out now. Gib, it must be really nice to have such an amazing person in your life."

Gib's confused expression never left his face, at least until he smiled and nodded. Something told me he'd just learned something about his foster mom.

After the gala was over, I escorted Mom back to her hotel, and was about to leave when she asked me to join her in her room for a few moments.

I sighed, but agreed, thinking she was going to get on my case again about not having kids. However, when we were seated, she said, "I am rather impressed with Gibbon Ridley. It appears he has a good head on his shoulders."

I nodded, not knowing where this was going.

"Oh, honey, don't act like you aren't head over heels for that man."

"Mom, we aren't... well, I'm not sure what we are yet. We only just admitted we both feel the same about each other. So, don't... well, I'm not sure you have anything to..."

I stopped talking. I was babbling, because things were still too new to know what to say.

"You have feelings, though?" Mom asked in her no-nonsense way.

"I have for a while, but Mom, don't make a big deal out of this. We're about to begin our residencies, and we both know we'll be too busy to do much other than work."

"But, you're doing your residency in Tennessee?" she asked.

"Yeah, Nashville, you know that."

"And he is doing his close to his hometown?" She said it like a question, but the look on her face made me understand it really wasn't one.

"You're blowing this up." I stood to go.

"No, don't go," she said. "Honey, I'm concerned. Lord knows I didn't want you to follow in your father's footsteps, the life of a doctor is intense and never-ending, but since you are, I just wanted to check and make sure you aren't getting yourself in over your head."

"Why, because I like Gib and am doing my residency in Nashville?"

She nodded, and I had to repress the same frustration I'd felt when Gib had basically wondered the same thing.

"Mom, I'm not doing my residency in Tennessee because Gib is there. If you want the truth, I'm doing it in Nashville, because Dad *isn't* there. Well, that's not entirely true either. I liked the hospital. It's huge, and it has a lot of moving parts, but when I visited, it was so real, not like the designer hospitals I'd interviewed at before. If I'm going to do this doctor thing, and after the work it took to graduate, I sure as hell intend to do this doctor thing, I want to be somewhere I'm making a real difference."

"And Gib being close by is just a coincidence?" she asked, and I could see she knew I wasn't being totally honest.

I began pacing the room. "Mostly, Mom," I said, letting my exasperation out in a sigh. "Okay, I admit I applied for a residency in Tennessee, because Gib was going to be down there, and I thought it'd be nice to be close to him, but I did like the place when I visited. If I hadn't, I promise, I would've turned it down."

She stood up, stopped my pacing by taking my hand, and then kissed my forehead like she used to do when I was little. "Then, I'm not going to worry about it any longer. I like Gib and I'm very impressed with his family. The fact he pulled himself up and managed to get through medical school. His foster mom filled me in on his resolve... well, that impressed me even more. But, since I'm your mother, and I love you and it's my job to look out for you, no matter how old you get, I will only ask you to make sure you take care of that sweet heart of yours."

With that, she pulled back, and said, "Now, go be with your friends. Since I have to fly out to Paris the day after tomorrow, I'm going to turn in soon. I hate jet lag, and when I'm not well rested, it kicks my butt."

I smiled, kissed her cheek, and pulled her into a hug. "Mom, you drive me crazy, but I love you."

She chucked. "I know, baby. Now go away." She playfully shoved me toward the door.

Mom was always like that. She never stood in the way of me being with my friends, or even my father and his family. Mostly, she wanted what was best for me, and for that, I would always be thankful.

Partying with my friends ended up with the four of us sitting in Fiona's dorm room watching Disney movies, while she and Alexi painted their toenails, and Gib and I cuddled on the sofa. "You know—" I said to him randomly after the thought hit me, "—if you hadn't been so standoffish, we could've been snuggling like this every night for the past few years."

He chuckled. "You were sort of busy dating every guy on campus."

"Well, at first, but not for a long time." I pouted.

Gib leaned over and kissed me, causing Fiona and Alexi to proclaim we needed to get a room.

"Shut up. You're just jealous," I said, before I announced that we should all make a pact to meet up every year, to at the very least, party and spend quality time together. Despite the fact we were all about to get carried away into our residencies, we owed it to ourselves to keep our Apple Fritter Gang friendship going.

"Yes!" Fiona said. "We really should. Let's agree to meet one year from today. Our first time should be at my family's summer home on Martha's Vineyard. They told me they won't be there next spring, because now my baby sister graduated from high school, they're going to spend next year in the South of France."

"Perfect, let's all agree to meet at Martha's Vineyard to celebrate the first anniversary of our graduation," I said.

Fiona and Alexi nodded, while Gib shook his head. "Y'all are the most silver-spoon people I know."

Gib rarely ever said anything about our being privileged, but I could tell he was teasing. "What? You won't come?" I asked, and he chuckled.

"Please, what poor country boy would pass up a chance to spend a week in Snootyville Vineyard?"

Alexi laughed. "Is Gib snubbing us?"

He chuckled. "No, not really. I'm just giving you some grief. It's good for you. Maybe it'll keep you humble."

"As if," I said, and he began tickling me.

When he stopped, he kissed the top of my head. "I'm in. Hell, you know how much time we've spent together these past few years. I can't imagine what it's gonna be like not seeing you all every day."

That put a damper on our evening. I didn't think any of us had really thought about that. In just a few short weeks, we would all be tucked into our new lives. Given how close we'd all become, it seemed almost impossible to imagine.

Seventeen

Gib

AFTER GRADUATION, I FLEW home to spend some downtime with my family. Allen would've come with me, but his father intervened, saying he was expected to join the family vacation to the Mediterranean, since there would be no time for a trip that long once his residency started.

It was fine, though. I enjoyed spending time with my nieces. The babies were getting much more interactive and had even begun crawling, which just meant they were in the middle of everything. I had no idea how quickly a toddler could get their little hands around someone's heart. I adored my niece. I loved the babies too, but Chrissy didn't give me much time to spend with them, and I could tell Olivia and Chase were beyond happy to have someone to help mitigate her jealousy.

Miss Margaret, the small businesswoman extraordinaire, who'd neglected to say anything about her past career, was shy when I brought up what I'd learned about her. Of course, I made a big production of it one Sunday after we'd returned home from church, so she had to tell us all.

She ended up shrugging it off. "Oh, that's nothing special," she responded as she put food out for lunch.

"That's not true now, is it?" Chase asked, and both Olivia and I turned toward him. He was the least likely of any of us to confront Miss Margaret. "The more I researched you, the more I learned that you, Miss Margaret Latham, were a superstar."

Miss Margaret blushed deeply, then stood tall, like she always did when she would hear no more of our nonsense, and began giving orders about the food. Some things never changed, no matter how old we got.

When Olivia, Chase and the kids left that evening, I sat across from the woman I realized I barely knew, and said, "You've kept huge parts of yourself from us, and before you get upset with me, I know we've done the same to you. I'd like to change all that now, Miss Margaret. We *are* family, after all."

She eyed me for a long time before she nodded. "Agreed, but to be honest, that was my past. I sold the company when my sister was diagnosed. She had you three hellions, who took everything she had to keep you from killing yourselves, so it was easier to let all that go. Besides, I mopped up with the sale." She chuckled to herself.

"That's why you could afford to send me to Harvard." It was more of a statement than a question, but I still needed confirmation. She nodded and I let out a breath. "I've been so afraid that you spent your retirement savings on my education. I'm still worried. I didn't really think much about it until I was halfway through, then I knew if I quit, you'd kill me."

She chuckled. "I made a lot of money from that sale, Gibbon. I also invested in three high-profile tech companies, including Amazon, so no, baby, you don't need to worry about me."

That was the first time Miss Margaret had called me baby, and it shocked me even more than learning I'd been raised by a business genius.

We sat together quietly in the formal Victorian parlor for a long time, listening to the ticking of the grandfather clock. Finally, I cleared my throat and asked what Olivia, Chase, and I had been dying to ask since the night Miss Margaret came out to us. "So, you gonna tell us about your significant other?" I asked.

Miss Margaret's eyes narrowed as she turned her attention to me, and I almost laughed at how quickly she switched back to the matriarch we'd always known. I could see her wrestling with internal conflicts that would've told me to mind my own business just a few years earlier.

"No," she simply said, and got up and left the room. It took every ounce of my will to keep from laughing out loud. At that moment, I realized not only how much I enjoyed getting my foster mom's dander up, but also how much I loved her.

Miss Margaret's personal life wasn't the only surprise she'd sprung on me recently. She'd allowed me to use an old truck that had belonged to Mr. Simmons when I'd been home from Harvard, and when I'd gotten my residency, she'd given me the old thing. I loved it like I would a new truck.

I suspected Miss Margaret had given me the truck, because she knew I'd feel a connection to Mr. and Mrs. Simmons every time I drove it, which I did. There was nothing sweet and cuddly about Miss Margaret, but she showed us love in her own ways, and I felt that when driving the old truck.

EIGHTEEN

ALLEN

I HAD TO FORCE myself not to whine about being away from Gib, just as we'd started something between us. We spoke for a full three hours on the phone the day before I flew to Greece with my dad.

Family vacations had been the bane of my existence for as long as I could remember. My dad had twisted my arm, as he always did, or I'd have avoided going altogether. My brother Lance hated it as much as I did, but then, he hated me too.

Since becoming a teenager, he'd become a lot more of a jerk, and now he was about to turn eighteen, he was beyond horrible to be around.

"Hey, wanna go parasailing with me?" I asked, trying anything to get through the gruff exterior that was my brother while we were below decks on our chartered boat.

"Fuck you," he said, and turned to leave the room. *God, our relationship never has had any hope.*

Before I could stop myself, I turned on him. "You know what? Fuck you too!" I said, surprising him. "Lance, you're a fucking jackass!" I left him standing there, and went up top to where Dad and Kassidy were.

Despite liking Kassidy's company, I would've much rather spent the summer with Gib and his family. I mean, the weeks spent cruising the Greek islands were amazing. I woke up, drank fresh-squeezed orange juice, took a swim in the Mediterranean, then if we were moored off one of the islands, I'd take a hike to explore, usually alone, but sometimes with Kassidy.

I chuckled to myself when I thought about what Gib would've said about living in the lap of luxury, and being upset that I wasn't hanging out in the middle of West Tennessee with him. I was sure he'd have called me entitled at the very least. What he didn't understand, though, was how much I wanted him. How much I craved being a part of his life.

The vacation passed quickly enough, and as soon as the plane landed, I grabbed a taxi to my mom's place to pack for my new life in Tennessee. Gib lived only an hour from Nashville, and the clinic where he'd be doing his residency was even closer. While floating in the Mediterranean, I'd decided to head to Nashville early to find a place to rent between the hospital and his clinic, and then talk him into living with me.

Yes, I knew it was a long shot. No, I didn't care. I'd spent several excruciating years pining for Gibbon Ridley, so I'd be damned if I didn't do everything in my power to keep that man close to me.

Mom's company owned a hotel outside Nashville, so I immediately booked myself into the largest suite, and began my housing search. I knew I'd be spending long hours working at the hospital, and I had to assume Gib would be doing the same. I'd looked the place up and found it served around thirty thousand patients, which was large for a publicly funded clinic that served mostly rural communities.

Although he'd never have the same sort of hours I would at the hospital, Gib had already told us when he got the residency assignment that he'd be on duty nearly every Saturday, and an on-call backup most of the time. So, I knew I had to have a place not far for either one of us, if I had a chance of talking him into moving in with me.

As luck would have it, I wasn't able to find any rentals located between our residency programs, but I did find a four-bedroom home for sale in a tiny town just west of Nashville.

I needed more than hopes and dreams to purchase a house, though, so with a mixture of excitement and uncertainty, I called my mom.

"Mom, it's so much cheaper than a condo near the hospital, and it's in a small town on the outskirts of the city. Best thing, though, is it's just a short drive to the hospital."

"Sounds like it's perfect. Besides, now you're in your residency, you'll want some permanence, I'm sure," she said.

"So, you don't mind if I use grandpa's college fund to pay for it?" I asked. That, of course, was the big question.

"Honey, that's your money. Your grandparents put that in a trust when you were still in diapers. It's yours to do with as you wish."

I smiled. "Thanks, Mom. Want to see pictures of the house?"

The rest of our conversation was me talking about what I wanted to do with the place, which I secretly thought would be perfect for Gib and me. Mom's encouragement gave me the extra push I needed to take the next step.

I took part of the money my grandparents had set aside for my education, which I hadn't had to spend thanks to my undergraduate scholarship, and Dad paying for medical school, and I put in an offer. Then, I checked out of the hotel and headed west toward Gib and his family.

The drive gave me plenty of time to conceive a plan of how to woo my boyfriend—*God, I loved calling him that*—into moving in with me.

Nineteen

Gib

I'D STARTED MY RESIDENCY one week before Allen showed up. I embraced him the second he got out of his car, and kissed him right there in front of God and everybody. I no longer cared what anyone thought about my relationship with another man. I was head over heels for the guy, and that was all that mattered.

We were just getting ready for supper when Olivia and Chase brought the girls over to join us. Of course, it was utter madness with the little ones. Olivia was carrying Chrissy, and Chase held a squirming baby in each arm.

The second Chrissy saw Allen, she shrugged out of her mom's arms and dashed into his. He barely had time to brace himself before she barreled into him.

"Uncle Allen!" she exclaimed, causing him to blush.

When he looked helplessly at me, I shrugged, and whispered, "She calls everyone she likes uncle or aunt. Welcome to the club."

Chrissy was nothing but demanding, so seeing that Olivia was enjoying the break, I took her from Allen and wandered into the kitchen to help put out the supper Miss Margaret had cooked for us.

Olivia and Chrissy each took turns asking Allen a hundred questions during our meal.

"It must be quite a change for you moving to Tennessee. How are you getting settled in Nashville?" Olivia asked.

Allen only had a moment to respond, before Chrissy asked, "Will you come visit us?"

I chuckled as both Chrissy and Olivia took turns putting Allen on the spot. Those two really were carbon copies.

When we'd finished supper, I helped load the kids into Olivia's car, and hugged her and Chase before they went home to tuck the kids in for the night. Normally, I would've gone with them, but not with Allen here.

I loaded the dishwasher while Miss Margaret showed Allen his room, which, incidentally, was a floor down from mine. The woman might have come out as a lesbian and was cool about my relationship with Allen, but she was still Miss Margaret, and there'd be no shenanigans under her roof until we were married.

For that reason, after Miss Margaret had retired to her sitting room, Allen and I walked up the road toward the old barn hill.

Olivia and Chase had hired an architect to design their new home on the property, but when they told Miss Margaret, she talked them into taking over the Victorian from her.

Probably because she wanted them to take over the house, Miss Margaret admitted she was ready to move to Franklin, just south of Nashville, where her girlfriend lived. It was still so strange that she'd admitted to us that she was a lesbian.

Regardless, with my permission and insistence that I'd be turning my ownership of the house over to them, they'd given up on the old barn hill, and decided to move into the sprawling home sometime in the fall.

Allen and I climbed up the steep hill, and when I showed him the hidden spot in the corner of the old barn's foundation, we made out like teenagers, until my butt fell asleep sitting on the concrete, then we stood up and leaned against the old stone walls, just holding each other, enjoying being together again.

Our arms were still wrapped around each other when Allen broke the silence, and shocked the hell out of me. "I bought a house," he burst out.

"What?" I asked, still drowsy from all the snuggling. "A house?"

He nodded. "Yeah, the rent in Nashville is ridiculous, and all I could find were one-bedroomed places I didn't want, so I bought a house outside of town."

"Okay, where at?" I asked, confused why he'd brought up the subject all of a sudden.

"Halfway between your clinic and my hospital."

"Aah," I said, the truth finally dawning on me. "You're trying to make it so we can spend more time together. Smart thinking."

He nodded and after a moment, asked, "So, where are you going to live?"

I shrugged. "Well, I had planned on driving back and forth from here, but Olivia and Chase are taking over the Victorian now Miss Margaret is moving. I talked to a former intern from the clinic, and he has a trailer I can rent until I get settled."

"A trailer? Like where the rednecks live?" he asked, causing me to laugh.

"Well, more than just rednecks live in trailers." I cleared my throat, trying not to laugh again. "This one is pretty redneck, though, I have to admit."

"No way, why?" he asked, shaking his head.

"'Cause, I'm never going to be there other than to sleep. On weekends, I'll end up either coming home to be with Olivia, Chase, and the girls, or... I was sorta hoping I'd be spending time with you."

That made Allen smile. "Wanna come with me tomorrow to see the house? It's less than an hour from here."

"Sure," I said. I'd already planned to spend the rest of the week with him.

We walked back and cuddled in my room, until we heard Miss Margaret deliberately walking down my hallway, which was on the other side of the house from hers. "Guess that's your cue to go to your own bedroom." I chuckled.

"Guess so," he said, cringing.

The minute he was gone, my heart was saddened at the loss. We hadn't had the chance to do anything other than kiss since we'd both confessed our feelings for one another. That was something I desperately wanted to remedy, and soon.

The next morning, we left early, so we could meet Allen's realtor at the house by nine o'clock. I was amazed at how quaint the place was. The master bedroom was a nice size, while the other bedrooms were smaller, but perfect for raising a family.

It had a distinct nineteen-seventies Brady Bunch feel, but the previous owner had renovated it beautifully, modernizing, but retaining its midcentury elements.

I guess I wasn't surprised that Allen would be living in a comfortable home while doing his residency. His family was loaded, after all. However, when I compared the house to the old, shabby trailer I'd be staying in, I couldn't help but feel a little envious.

After we left, we headed to the next town over, and had a late breakfast at a cute little café. "What do you think of the house?" Allen asked.

"It's beautiful, perfectly renovated..." I let my words hang in the air as I struggled to come to terms with my envy.

"So..." he asked, sounding hopeful for some reason.

I arched my eyebrow at the handsome man sitting across from me. "So, what?" I asked, confused about what he was getting at.

"So, you crazy nut, are you willing to move in with me? It's just under half an hour from your clinic. You can easily do the drive…"

Allen was still talking, but my brain had turned to mush. Move in with him? Hell, we weren't even dating, at least not yet. We were still in the making-out stage. How the hell was I going to live with him? All my fears were being stirred up again, and I was finding it hard to breathe.

Luckily, the waitress came over and filled my coffee mug, giving me a moment to take a long, hot sip and gather my thoughts.

Allen had stopped talking and was staring at me. He had the same concerned expression he'd had when I'd reacted badly to him taking a residency so close to me. "You're freaking out."

"Well," I hedged, managing to get myself together. "Of course, I'm freaking out, Allen. We just started this. We haven't even slept together. How are we going from a first date to moving in with each other?"

"Gib, we aren't new. We've been friends for years now. I care about you more than I have any other man. I care about you like family, Gib."

"I care about you too, and just like you, I consider you more than a friend. You're like family to me, and that's why this scares me so much. What if I say yes, then you decide you don't want to date me any longer? What if someone better comes along? I've got to figure out how to keep my heart separated from all that, so I can still be your friend."

Allen continued to stare silently at me, his expression unreadable. But, the years of friendship were telling me he was frustrated. When the waitress brought us our food, he sighed and shook his head. "If that's how you're doing this relationship, by holding part of your heart back from me, then, Gib, it's not going to work. Can't you see I'm all in?" he asked, wiping at a couple tears that had slipped from his eyes.

"Allen, you're... you are such an eligible bachelor, you've dated so many guys. Even this morning, the realtor was flirting with you, and we're in the middle of Podunkville, Tennessee." It took me a moment to find the right words, and I sighed out of frustration, before continuing, "Baby, I know it's possible that you and I might be the forever kind of relationship. I think that'd be easier for me than for you. I've never cared much for dating or screwing around with other guys. I'm perfectly happy nesting with just one man. In fact, I think I'm lucky as hell, considering where I'm from and where I'm doing my residency, that I have a man like you interested in me at all. But, I think we need time. Don't you?"

My question hung in the air when Allen glanced around, but didn't answer, then resumed eating his greasy Southern breakfast. The agitated look on his face told me he had more to say on the subject, but was holding back, since our conversation was beginning to draw the attention of other diners. Finally, when I dropped down a twenty, which more than covered our meals and the tip, we both got up and walked toward his vehicle.

The moment he got in and closed his door, Allen turned to me, clearly extending an olive branch, and said, "Okay, show me the trailer you're going to be living in."

I nodded, not at all sure what he was expecting, and we drove the thirty minutes to the small town where I was doing my residency. The trailer was less than a mile from the clinic, which I thought was perfect, since I was on-call most of the time and could get there at a moment's notice. As we headed up a hill from the downtown area, I pointed out the gravel driveway leading up into the forested area where the trailer sat.

We pulled up to the old trailer in silence. Allen got out and stared open-mouthed at the ancient, broken-down thing. "You'd choose to live here over living with me?" he asked, the hurt clear in his voice. "How the hell are you going to live in this thing for three years?"

I walked over and pulled him into an embrace, which I could tell he wanted to resist, but, thankfully, didn't.

"Yeah, if it means we both have a real chance of developing a relationship, one that isn't dependent on my living with you, I'll happily live here."

When we pulled apart, Allen walked up to the trailer and turned the knob. He'd correctly assumed that an old trailer out in the middle of nowhere like this wouldn't be locked. He walked in, not even asking if anyone lived there, then looked around at the dated furnishings.

The truth was, the trailer was ugly inside and out, but it was more than adequate for my needs. It was also neat as a pin. The former clinic intern I was renting it from had been married to a neat freak.

Even now, having sat vacant for over two months, the trailer still smelled clean. Of course, I knew Allen wouldn't see any of that.

"Okay, I get it," he finally said. "But, you have to promise me that once we've been together long enough for you to see how serious I am about us, you'll leave this dump and move in with me."

I chuckled before going to him and leaning down to kiss his adorable mouth. "I promise that once I'm sure it will be good for us both, I'll consider moving into your fancy country house, and out of my hillbilly trailer."

"By the way..." he said, looking around, "...where's the still?"

I laughed out loud, because, no joke, the owner literally kept a distilling setup in the shed out back. Damned if I was going to admit that to Allen, though.

For now, I was just happy to have him accept that we could take things at a normal, healthy speed. I needed that, even though I was already sure my heart was his, and always would be.

TWENTY

ALLEN

SUMMER QUICKLY FADED INTO fall, although the humidity didn't seem to get the memo. I'd started my residency in a flurry of activity. Clearly, every pediatrician over me had taken it upon themselves to push the Harvard resident to the brink of insanity.

I loved the work. I even loved the challenges. What I didn't love was that I never got to see Gib. He was busy too, although nowhere near as busy as me. He ended up bringing me midnight lunches during the weekends when I was pulling sixteen-hour shifts, because of some infraction one of the other doctors had invented. I honestly regretted buying the house, because, frankly, I was never there. Most of the minimal sleep I did get was in an empty hospital room.

Though few and far between, visits from Gib were amazing and romantic. God, I missed him. On the rare weekend off, I would all but beg Gib to stay with me at the house. Luckily, he never said no, and we'd spend the time cuddled up, while I slept off the exhaustion from weeks of working eighty-plus hours.

When we did venture out together, Gib spoiled me delightfully. "Hey—" he said out of the blue one weekend. "—you need to taste real barbeque."

"Verses virtual barbeque?" I asked, and got an eye roll from him.

"Come on, I want you to taste it, the real stuff."

I chuckled, but I could never say no to him. He'd called Olivia and Chase, and we met them and the girls at a real dive in the middle of nowhere. The smoke coming out of the building was definitely a cancer risk, so I persuaded everyone to sit outside on the picnic tables. Being fall, the leaves were changing to beautiful shades of red and amber, but it was still warm enough to eat outside.

When I bit into the sandwich, I totally understood why we were here. The flavors hit me instantly and smoky pork melted in my mouth. Gib encouraged me to try a vinegar-based hot sauce, which I would've never put on my food, but somehow it enhanced the flavor of the pulled pork.

"Now you are tasting real barbeque," Olivia said, and I looked at her questioningly.

"Because, other pulled pork isn't barbeque?"

"No, it's Yankeeque," Chase said, making Gib and Olivia chuckle.

I loved that Olivia and Chase were giving me the business like they usually did Gib, making me feel like I was really becoming part of this family.

Gib delighted in treating me to uniquely Southern fare, probably just to hear the uncontrollable, obscene moans I made when devouring delicious food.

I kissed Gib thoroughly. "I appreciate you so much, Gib. With all that's going on, I..."

"You're freakishly busy," he finished for me. "Don't apologize, we knew it would be this way."

I pulled him into a hug, and had to fight every impulse not to tell him how much I loved him. I'd been in love with Gib long before we became boyfriends. I'd told him before we started dating, but that had been a different time. Things were... well, they were domestic now. No more classes, just the real world of treating the sick, and trying to get enough sleep to get up the next day and do it all again. I knew he'd freak out if I said the three little words right now, though. I needed to bide my time until he was ready to hear them again.

Gib had been stuck on-call one of the rare Saturdays I was off, so I went to stay with him in his trailer. It was winter and so cold out that he was afraid the pipes were going to freeze. He got a call around seven that night, and before he left, he told me not to turn off the water. "It has to run to keep from freezing."

I could understand why, it was freezing cold in the trailer. The previous owner had kept a wood-burning stove in the living room, but they'd taken it with them when they moved, so Gib was relying on the old trailer's furnace to keep the place warm. It clearly wasn't working. I decided then I was putting my foot down.

It was ridiculous that Gib was living here when I had a perfectly cozy home that sat empty most of the time. Hell, even if he was on call, the house was only twenty-five minutes from here. If there were an actual emergency, his patients should go to an emergency room, not call him. In fact, it sounded like he was meeting a family at the clinic tonight more to convince them to take their baby to the ER than to treat her.

I ended up falling asleep with every blanket I could find piled on top of me to stay warm. I didn't hear Gib when he came in, but he slipped into bed behind me, waking me up with his freezing cold body.

I should've chastised him, but even cold, his body felt like sheer perfection snuggled into mine.

I turned over, still shivering despite the mound of blankets on top of me, as I cuddled in close. "You're moving in with me tomorrow."

He didn't say anything, just flipped the bedside lamp on, and stared at me with those intense hazel-colored eyes of his.

"Good, you've got enough sense not to argue," I said, and rolled back over. "Now, come here and help warm me up, this is ridiculous!" I snuggled my bum into his crotch.

"I'm..."

"Shh," I said, stopping his argument before he could get started. We ended up falling asleep spooning. Frankly, that was the only way either of us stayed warm that night. Although I cursed the bitter cold, I was thankful it left no question about Gib finally moving in with me.

Twenty-One

Gib

To be honest, I'd thought about asking Allen if he was still interested in cohabitating. Unfortunately, the trailer was getting colder by the day. I'd almost bought a wood stove, but decided against it after treating a family for severe burns suffered when their trailer burned to the ground.

Beyond not wanting to freeze, though, Allen and I were getting closer all the time. The transition from friends to boyfriends had been an easy one. I had figured Allen would be cuddly. He had been even when we were just friends, but now we'd crossed over to sleeping together and making love, he seemed to be touching me all the time.

Having been raised in an environment that wasn't big on physical contact, it took some getting used to. Now that I had, though, I craved having him within reach, which didn't happen near enough, because of his insane work schedule.

"Hey," I said, surprised when Allen showed up at my trailer out of the blue one Saturday.

"Hey, yourself," he said, and looked sheepish. "Sorry, I missed you and didn't want to give you a reason to tell me I shouldn't come."

I chuckled and kissed him. "I wouldn't have told you not to come. I missed you too. Actually, you have great timing. Wanna join me for lunch? I was just about to go into town for a burger at Lucille's Diner."

Before he could answer, my phone buzzed with a call from the clinic. We both knew what that meant.

When I hung up, I shrugged. "Duty calls. Sorry."

"I knew you were on-call. Go on, and I'll run over to Lucille's and get us both a burger. You can eat yours when you get home."

I kissed him and agreed, although I knew the situation I was heading into, and that I wouldn't be back any time soon.

When I got home, Allen was buried under a mountain of blankets. I didn't really mind sleeping in the cold. Even with the new insulation Miss Margaret had installed in the old Victorian when she'd moved in, there had still been plenty of drafts. My and Chase's bedroom had been particularly cold since we were on the north side of the house, and the wind beat against our bedroom window in the winter.

When I crawled into bed and snuggled up to Allen's warmth, I was once again filled with happiness. When I had Allen in my arms, the world felt right. I was about to drift off when Allen turned in my arms, and announced that I was moving in with him. I opened my mouth to agree, and he must've thought I was going to argue, because he shushed me. I couldn't help but pull his small muscular body tighter into mine.

It took everything in me not to say then and there just how much I loved him. Luckily, within seconds, I was asleep, preventing me from saying it in the heat of the moment.

The next morning, I woke up to Allen's cussing, and went to find him trying to light the gas stove in the kitchen. "This place is a freaking death trap," he complained, when the flames jumped up almost to his face.

I walked over and slipped my arms around him. "Why aren't you still in bed?" I asked, and he sighed.

"'Cause, I wanted to make you breakfast for a change. It seems that with my crazy schedule, you're always waiting on me."

"Mmm, but I love doing things for you," I whispered into his ear, sending a shiver down Allen's body.

I kissed his neck. "Why don't we make breakfast together... at least after I go pee!"

I rushed off to the bathroom. When I came back, I began frying the bacon in the old cast-iron skillet that had been left behind by the previous occupant.

After breakfast, Allen told me to pack. "I'm taking you home with me, and no argument, hear me?"

I chuckled. "I'm not sure I like it when you're all bossy."

He wiggled his eyebrows, and said, "Experience says otherwise, but in all seriousness, Gib, you can't stay here in the cold. You'll end up getting hypothermia or something."

I chuckled. "I was going to ask you if the offer still stood, but you beat me to it."

"Of course, it still stands."

Allen came over and put his arms around me. "Gib, there is nothing I want more than to live with you. That's what I've wanted from day one. Besides, I think now that I've proven myself at the hospital, I'll have a little more time on my hands. I'd love to spend that free time with you."

"Yeah, me too. So... um... yeah, if you're really serious, I'd like to give that a try."

Allen smiled from ear to ear before kissing me soundly on the mouth. "Mmm, you've got bacon breath. I think I like bacon kisses."

"If you like that, I've got something even better," I teased as I drew Allen back to the bedroom.

TWENTY-TWO

ALLEN

G IB CALLED HIS LANDLORD, a doctor who now worked in practice just outside Nashville, and told him he'd be moving out. I could hear him laughing, saying he was surprised Gib lasted as long as he had in the cold. I just shook my head, and went to help move some of Gib's things, few as they were, into my car.

I helped him winterproof the pipes with antifreeze, then he closed up the trailer, hopefully never to return. Finally, he put his bike in the back of his old truck and followed me from the trailer of hell to my wonderful home, where the heater kept us warm, and we didn't have to leave the water running to keep the pipes from freezing.

Gib ended up moving in at the perfect time. Instead of my schedule getting easier, a bad bout of flu hit the Nashville area, meaning I was working pretty-much seven days a week at the hospital. Gib was working ridiculous hours too, but at least he had time to come home and keep the place from falling into total disrepair in my absence.

Despite the chaos, I was so happy to come home to Gib. Even if he was already asleep when I got home, it just felt so good crawling into bed with him. He'd often roll over, spoon my body, and tell me, "You feel so good..." before slipping back to sleep.

I texted Fiona and Alexi.

Me: *I finally get this man to move in with me, and I barely have time to see him.*

Fiona: *Hey, don't complain, at least you got someone to cuddle with.*

Alexi: *Truth, I barely have time to do anything other than hug my pillow.*

Then, I'd inevitably get a group text that included Gib.

Alexi: *Allen said you're neglecting your man.*

Gib: Allen is spoiled and works too much.

Me: Hey, I'm right here...

Fiona: Allen is a baby, we all know it, but Gib, stop neglecting your man.

God, I missed them.

By the end of April, I was totally burned out. The flu had been followed by an outbreak of whooping cough, which I'd somehow managed to catch. I gave my supervising physician the eye when she said it wasn't supposed to be that bad in adults. "Someone lied to you," I said as I burst into a fit of coughing.

Gib, ever the supportive boyfriend, teased me about it. "I'm telling you this is proof of what I've been saying for years, you are just a freaking overgrown kid."

I opened my mouth to tell him off when another cough hit me. "Ugh, you're an ass..." I said between coughs, and flipped him off.

The time away from the job had ended up being a godsend though. My supervising doctors reveled in saddling me, the Harvard boy, with extra work, but because I was out sick for a week, all that shit fell through the cracks. Fortunately, the head of pediatrics, the *other* Harvard boy and reason I'd gotten the residency to begin with, noticed how much I'd been doing.

When I was finally able to return, the place was totally different. When several of the pediatricians wouldn't look me in the eye, I figured things were going to get even worse. Being called into Dr. Jeffers's office didn't ease my suspicion.

"Son," he said, and I cringed, nervous anticipation almost debilitating me. "You've been given... higher than normal expectations, and despite that, your evaluations from staff and patients alike have been impeccable." I nodded along, waiting for the shoe to drop. "We've decided to give you an extra week off to compensate for the multiple ninety-five-hour weeks you've spent over the past few months. I know you're dedicated, but at this rate you're going to burn out."

I stared at Dr. Jeffers for several moments before it sank in that I was being praised, not getting into trouble. "Um... thank you, sir," I said, and shook his hand, then practically dashed out of his office before he could change his mind.

I noticed my work weeks following my return were significantly shorter. I seldom worked more than eighty hours, and there were a few weeks when I worked less than sixty. That was unheard of for a resident in a hospital that served a patient population like ours.

The pediatricians were also nicer to me all of a sudden. No one ever said why or what had happened, but I was guessing Dr. Jeffers had laid down the law. I spent my newfound freedom languishing in the sweet embrace of my boyfriend.

"Hey, can we go hiking Sunday?" I asked, needing to get away now I had an actual day off.

"Sure, let's go to Lookout Mountain. There are some nice hiking trails up there, and it's beautiful."

It took a little drive to get there, but the scenery was beyond words. You could see at least three states from some of the vistas.

That night, I lay snuggled into Gib, happier than I'd been in a long, long time. "I love Tennessee," I said. "It's so pretty here."

Gib kissed my neck and hummed his agreement. "Let's do this more often, okay?"

It was my turn to hum my agreement, and I had to bite my tongue not to blurt out how much I loved him.

TWENTY-THREE

GIB

I LOVED FAMILY PRACTICE. I mean, totally and completely loved it, and I felt like I was beginning to make a
real impact.

One Saturday after my shift, I was driving by the local
church when I saw a group of boys playing basketball
behind the building. One boy was clutching his ankle
and moaning, so I stopped to check on him. "You think
you broke it?" I asked him.

Through clenched teeth, he said, "It hurts real bad."

I called the nurse practitioner, and she agreed to open
the clinic back up, since I'd yet to be given a key. I
immediately set about x-raying his foot while the nurse
practitioner called the kid's mom, getting permission to
treat him.

His injury ended up being a sprain, but as a result,
I'd been automatically welcomed into the community.

The kid's dad was the pastor at the church where they were playing ball, and the family sang my praises. After that, the number of people who showed up at the clinic asking for me by name increased significantly.

Until that point in my residency, I'd spent a frustrating amount of time feeling like a glorified medical assistant. At first, the clinical director didn't want me to see that many patients, but considering we were pulling in more people who were actually insured for a change, he quickly changed his mind. "Gib—" he said one day, "—it's time for you to start seeing patients."

Brenda, our nurse practitioner who'd heard the whole exchange, looked over at me and quietly laughed. "It's about damned time," she said under her breath.

I loved every stressful moment. The busy days, the camaraderie between the staff, and becoming a trusted member in the community. If I hadn't already decided I wanted to work in a rural setting, I would've been set on it now. I knew I wanted to be a small-town doctor who could treat entire families and get to know them.

"So, what're you gonna do?" Brenda asked me when I shared my epiphany about wanting to stay in a clinic like this one.

"Probably get a fellowship in geriatrics," I said. "You know, most people who live in small towns are older. I could use more training to keep them healthy."

She just shrugged. "You know enough, but do what you think you need to. Whatever you decide to do next, Gib, stay the course. Small-town doctors are disappearing at an alarming rate, we need you," she said, before disappearing into a patient's room.

Allen's workload was twice mine. I felt bad for him, although he seemed to thrive in the high-pressure environment, so I just tried to support him, and let him know I was here if he needed me.

After Allen got sick, more probably because of stress than actual whooping cough, the hospital began to lighten up on him. Thank goodness, I'd had no idea how he was going to operate at that level of intensity much longer.

Our trip to Lookout Mountain was exactly what we both needed. Even if it was only for a few days, it was enough to fill both of our souls back up, so we could continue our hectic lifestyles. It also allowed us to bond more than we had in a long time.

Unfortunately, the moment we got back, things turned hectic again.

"Um, are you going to be home tonight?" I asked one evening, when I had research to do.

"Yeah, I'll be home. Why? Did you want to do something?"

I shrugged, and replied, "I sort of need to do some review research on HPV. I think we're seeing an epidemic and I wanted to be more versed on it before the epidemiologist shows up."

Allen nodded. "Cool, I'll fix dinner."

I nodded, feeling guilty. More time together should've been a good thing, considering we'd been friends before it became more, but we'd had such different lives for the past nine months, it felt weird for it to just be us, and I'd admit, I was having a hard time adjusting to just hanging out again.

The past year had been such a blur of work that our first graduation anniversary snuck up on both of us. Honoring our group pact to hang with Fiona and Alexi on Martha's Vineyard was a vacation we all needed. Allen had been given time off, so he didn't even have to ask for it. He just told them he was going to be gone and the date, and no one lifted an eyebrow.

For me, it wasn't quite so easy. I'd been working less than a year in my residency, so asking for a week off was something I had to work hard to explain. Eventually, it was Brenda who got my request pushed through.

I was free to join my boyfriend on vacation with our friends. The Apple Fritter Gang was getting back together, and I couldn't wait to see them.

Twenty-Four

Allen

GIB HAD BEEN FRETTING over Alexi and Fiona not being able to get away long enough to join us in Martha's Vineyard for our graduation reunion. I knew from talking to both of them they were both respected in their programs, and seriously doubted anyone would complain about them taking time off.

Fiona called the first week of May, confirming she and Alexi were set to join us. I told her we were free as well. It wasn't until right then that it sank in we were actually going to see each other again after almost a year apart.

This vacation would be good for Gib and me. Besides the trip to Lookout Mountain, we'd become so busy we had a hard time navigating our relationship. By no means were we struggling, but we were having difficulty adjusting to our work-life balance. Maybe a week with the four of us back together again was just what we needed to get back on track. At least, I secretly hoped so. I missed my friends, but more than anything, I missed the easy camaraderie I'd once had with Gib.

We flew out of Nashville early on Friday morning, and only had one layover in Chicago, so the plane wasn't crowded. I ended up falling asleep on Gib as he read a novel on his Kindle. When we finally arrived in Newark, Fiona and Alexi were there to pick us up for the six-hour drive to the Vineyard.

"Oh my god, you're here!" Alexi said as she pulled me into a hug, then did the same to Gib. Fiona came up behind her and hugged us both as well.

"We're so ready for a vacation," Fiona said, and it felt good that we were finally back together.

Although we were excited to see our friends, Gib and I fell asleep in the back seat as soon as we got on the road, and slept most of the way there. Just hearing the chatter from Fiona and Alexi was enough to comfort me, and I was still significantly behind on sleep.

Once we made it to Fiona's family's vacation home, we piled out of the car and headed in to claim our rooms. Gib stared at the enormous home for several seconds before shaking his head. All three of us waited to hear his comment. Instead, he just followed us into the house, his *rich people* comments held back for the time being.

Once we were settled in our room, Gib pushed me onto the bed and began kissing and tickling me. "Wait!" I yelled between giggles. "What's all this about?" I asked, when he finally let me go.

"I'm just happy. I know we all needed this break, but being with Fiona and Alexi just seems to feel right. I've missed them."

"Yeah, me too," I said, and leaned up to kiss him. "I've missed you too."

He nodded. "They did warn us in school that our residencies would be all-consuming."

"Yeah. I guess that's true," I said with a sigh. "It's only two more years, right?"

"Um, no. It's four more years for you, remember?" he said, laughing.

"I can't believe I signed up for two additional years. What was I thinking?"

"That you want to run the freaking hospital someday," he said, with what sounded like a note of pride.

"Yeah, well, is it too late to change my mind?"

He shrugged. "You love it, and you know it. Now come on, let's go find the girls and start this vacation right!"

What we found, however, was a shock to both of us. We walked down the stairs and out the back door just in time to see Fiona and Alexi pulling back from a kiss.

"Well, well," I said, making both of them jump. "Mind explaining when all this started?"

Alexi smiled, then said, "Well, it's sort of new."

I noticed Gib give Alexi a knowing look, and I figured there was more to it than I knew. Regardless, I continued to rib them. "So, how new?"

Fiona chuckled. "Only a few months. We got together over the New Year and then one thing led to another."

"About time," Gib said, and grabbed a beer out of Fiona's open cooler before plopping down in the Adirondack chair that faced the ocean.

"Hey," Fiona said, and popped him on the head as she walked by to get her own beer.

I looked at Alexi, and asked, "So, why didn't you tell us?"

Alexi just smirked at me. "Do you call to tell me when you and Gib are hooking up?"

I chuckled. "Well, I probably would if we actually had time to hook up."

Gib laughed along with the girls. Like it or not, that really was the current situation with us. Most of the time, when we were home, either I was sleeping, or he was being called away to handle some crisis. It didn't leave much room for romance.

Both Alexi and Fiona nodded, but I could tell they hardly related. Fiona was doing her residency in the same high-end plastic surgery clinic she'd interned at in Manhattan. They'd loved her before she even started, so she wasn't having to prove herself like I was.

Alexi was working for my dad, and he adored her. She laughed when I asked her if he gave her any grief about it, saying he and a couple other doctors had to force her to take time off.

Despite the differences in our new lives, we easily fell back into our friendship, as if no time had passed. We spent the evening laughing over swapped stories of our residency experiences.

As I listened to Gib, I realized just how little he and I had been communicating these past few months. I knew a lot of that had to do with my work situation, but I also had to acknowledge how little I'd done to prompt him to talk about his days. As we all laughed at some of the patient antics he recounted, I resolved to be more inquisitive about his life, and to share more of mine with him.

TWENTY-FIVE

GIB

M Y GOD, I NEEDED this week. I'd almost backed out when my clinical director balked at my vacation request, but I was glad I didn't. In my chats with Fiona, I had caught wind of the fact she and Alexi were spending more time together, and I guessed something more was developing between them.

It was sweet that they'd finally found their footing in the romance department. Alexi was clearly in love with Fiona, and there'd been times I suspected Fiona also craved more, but was too shy to pursue it.

That night, Fiona and Allen went walking along the beach when Alexi and I volunteered to clean up after supper. Mostly, I wanted to have time alone with her to get the deep and dirty gossip.

"So," I began, tossing the sponge into the sink after wiping down the counter. "You gonna tell me what spurred this on?"

Alexi laughed. "I wondered how long it'd take you to corner me."

I put my hands in the air. "No cornering here, just curious."

Alexi put the last glass in the dishwasher, and turned it on before turning to me and sighing. "It's been overwhelming. Believe it or not, Fiona made the first move. I was content just being friends, but she'd gotten tipsy at a New Year's Eve party we'd gone to together. When the clock struck twelve, she leaned in and kissed me, tongue and all."

"Shit, really?" I asked, shocked.

"Oh yeah, and I was willing to pass it off as too much wine, when just a few minutes later, she confessed she'd had feelings for me throughout high school, college, *and* med school."

"Why did it take her so long to admit it?" I asked.

"Fear. Mostly, I think she was afraid of her parents. They aren't the easiest to manage, even when you're straight and popping out babies. In fact, her sister is engaged to a high roller on Wall Street, and her mother is giving her all sorts of grief about it."

"Has she told them you two are dating?"

Alexi shook her head. "No, but they were at the party when Fiona stuck her tongue down my throat."

"Really? Wow. So, what have they said?"

"Nothing. Absolutely nothing, not that she seems to care. This position she's got has changed her. She's more confident. She doesn't need validation from her parents like she used to. It's sort of sexy to see, actually."

I laughed. "I'm guessing everything about her is sexy to you at the moment."

"No doubt," Alexi teased, and ribbed me with her elbow. "So, tell me about how you and Allen are doing."

I smiled and it was more strained than I meant it to be. "We're fine. Navigating his intense residency, but fine."

"They're giving him a lot of grief, aren't they?" she asked.

"They were. He blossomed under the pressure, though. It just didn't give us much time to be a couple. Now he's got more normal hours, though, we're struggling to find our footing."

"You sure you aren't doing your *pull away to protect your heart* thing?"

I stared at her and thought for a moment before I sighed and shrugged. "Maybe. I keep thinking it's just a matter of time before he decides to head back up here. My heart doesn't want to be completely shattered when he does."

Alexi watched me briefly before she shook her head. "Gib, I can't tell you what Allen will do. It shocked all of us that he chose Nashville for his residency. He seemed more like the kind of guy who'd want to spend his off time on a beach, or chasing beach bunnies."

I knew what she meant and completely agreed with her. Allen was sexy as hell. His tight, slim body was made for swimming in the ocean, which he planned on doing during our trip.

"The issue is—" she continued, "—he went to Tennessee, and although I think he does love the hospital, Fiona and I both believe he went there mainly for you. Now, don't get that screwed-up look on your face, it isn't a bad thing. He seriously needed to do some growing up, and from the sound of it, this residency program is forcing him to do that. He also cares a lot about you. I mean, even now when he looks at you, his expression is like a puppy with a new owner." She chuckled at the analogy, and I couldn't argue with her. Allen treated me well, even though we sometimes didn't quite know how to deal with each other.

"I doubt he'll want to move back as long as you're with him," she added.

"My world is upside down, Alexi. I love the clinic. I love being back home with my family and getting to see my nieces. I'm also in love with Allen, but when I think about our lives, or what our lives might be like, I can't reconcile it. He's gonna want to be in some big hospital, and I'm gonna want to be in a clinic similar to where I'm at now." I waited a moment as I gathered my thoughts. "I doubt I'll ever want to leave Tennessee again, so what does that mean for a relationship with him?"

Alexi drew me into a hug and when she pulled back, she said, "You are the biggest overthinker I've ever known. If you love him and he loves you, then you'll figure it out. I mean, you might have to compromise a bit, but in the long run, trust me, there's very little two

Harvard-trained doctors can't figure out if they really want to."

I smiled. If anyone were looking at our relationship from the outside, it would seem like the two of us had a perfect setup. We'd both gone to the same medical school, both became doctors. The reality was, though, beyond school, lifestyles among doctors could be quite different. Would Allen and I be able to overcome those differences?

I followed Alexi out to the porch, and we sat facing the now-dark ocean, its smell wafting over us on the gentle breeze. We sat silently, simply listening to the waves crashing on the shore. Alexi and I had always had the kind of friendship where we could sit for hours without speaking. Of course, in the past, we were usually both studying, but this felt okay too. No matter what happened, she and I would always be close friends. I figured it wasn't too much of a stretch to see that Allen and I had a chance at remaining close too... even if it was *only* as friends.

Twenty-Six

Allen

T HE WEEK WAS PERFECT. For the most part, Gib and Alexi lay on a blanket absorbing the sun, or watching Fiona and I dash in and out of the cold ocean, laughing at our antics. Alexi and Gib spent a lot more time together than I remembered them doing in school. It was nice to see, especially since Fiona and I had always been close. One night when we were hit with a storm, we all sat inside watching *Mama Mia*, laughing at the similarities between the friends in that story and us. Gib teased me, saying I was Meryl Streep's character. "Of course," I teased back. "You *would* think of yourself as Sam Carmichael."

"What, you don't think I'm a daddy Sam Carmichael equivalent? Or are you comparing me to Pierce Brosnan?"

"Either way, you're much sexier," I said as I leaned back into him on the sofa, and his arms tightened around me.

Way too soon, it was time to head back to Tennessee. Alexi and Fiona drove us back to the airport, and as we flew away from our friends, I sighed and told Gib how much I hoped we never stopped getting together like this. When he looked at me funny, I pushed him to tell me what he was thinking.

"Don't you think you'll eventually wanna go back to New York?" he asked.

I shrugged. "I don't really know, to be honest. I don't have much left for me there, except maybe our friends. Mom sold her brownstone and is living full-time in Paris now. Dad isn't quite as much of a jerk as he used to be, but I doubt I'll ever want to live too close to him, so I don't know. It's not like I feel myself being called back or anything."

"Do you think you'd like to stay in Tennessee?" he asked. He wasn't exactly asking me to stay with him forever, but I could feel his discomfort talking about it. Even though we were sitting in the middle of a crowded flight, it was time we had this conversation. Gib was putting his heart out there in his own way, and I couldn't afford to screw this up with a wrong answer.

"Maybe. I mean, I know I love pediatrics... a lot more than I thought I would, actually." I chuckled. "I figured I'd just eventually work in administration, but I love the work I'm doing." I looked at him for a long moment, nearly getting lost in his beautiful hazel-colored eyes. "I don't know if it matters much to me where I'm at, Gib, as long as I'm doing what I love, and have the man I love in my life."

Love. I knew it was a loaded word. I'd told him last year that I loved him, but we hadn't brought it up since. Either my words or the moment was too much, because he remained silent and glanced away. I reached over, gently taking hold of his chin, and turned his face back toward me until we locked eyes again. "I love you, Gib. I have for a long time. I think it's time I start telling you that."

I was shocked to see a well of emotion my words had caused transform his expression. He swiped at an errant tear, and whispered, "I love you too, more than I know how to deal with."

Gib reacted to the huge smile that crossed my face by gifting me one to match. "No problem," I teased. "We can deal with it together. Besides, I think that's how it's supposed to work."

We happily held hands as we exited the plane, and drove back to our little house in the country. We both had to be back at work the next day, but had the rest of the day to snuggle into each other, and enjoy having found our footing once again.

Twenty-Seven

Gib

I T WAS ALMOST LIKE we'd never left. The day I got back to work, I had a schedule full of patients. More than usual, actually, because I'd been gone for a week.

Allen was back to working ridiculous hours, but never as bad as it'd been before he'd gotten sick. Despite that, we fell into a rhythm that worked for us. Seldom did we have more than a few hours together, but life somehow worked out anyway, especially since we were both working at communicating with each other better.

The months passed by quickly. When Allen was working long weekend shifts, I'd go back home to help with the nieces. Olivia and Chase had decided to enroll Chrissy in preschool that fall to help prepare her for attending kindergarten the following year.

Ruby and Margie were both in the full throes of the terrible twos. Olivia had recently gone back to work part-time, which meant the nanny Miss Margaret had hired ended up staying at the house full-time.

Miss Margaret had moved to Franklin, which surprisingly, Olivia mourned frequently, saying how strange it was living in the old Victorian without one of our foster moms there. She and Miss Margaret had really bonded over the raising of the girls. I knew more than anything Olivia was missing her relationship with the only mother she had left. Now that Miss Margaret wasn't the dictator she'd been when we were kids, I too had begun to think of her as a parent.

Allen and I usually had Sundays off together, so that was officially our day. Sometimes he'd go with me to visit the family, and we'd spend the night there. Most of the time, though, I'd spend Mondays with them, since I tended to have that day off too, then drive to the clinic on Tuesday mornings.

"I'm not going," I overheard Chrissy say as I spoke with Olivia on the phone one morning. Olivia had called me, exasperated and amused. "Uncle Gib is coming, and I want to see him!" Chrissy yelled in the background.

"Um, well, I can pick her up from preschool, if that helps," I offered. I could tell by her chuckling that Olivia was amused my niece could dictate my day, even though I wasn't there.

"Uncle Gib said that if you go to preschool, he'll pick you up... and even buy you an ice cream."

"Wait, Olivia, I didn't say ice cream! She'll be hyper as..."

"Yay!" Chrissy's shout of joy in the background told me I'd lost the argument. Hyper or not, I was buying her an ice cream.

In a roundabout way, that was how our new schedule began. Since Chrissy would be attending kindergarten the following year, we all agreed I'd pick her up from preschool at noon on Mondays, so she'd be used to going to school. It also meant she still had quality time with me when I was there.

The toddlers, well, they were a handful. I would've never thought it possible, but they were even more than Chrissy had been. I loved my Monday mornings helping get the girls situated as Olivia and Chase prepared for work before the nanny arrived. Olivia's new job was in Jackson, working with a foster-care organization that was new to the area.

"You'll bring firsthand experience," I told her, when she first told me about the job.

"Yeah, and I'm determined to make some positive changes." I knew she would too. Olivia was a powerful force when she put her mind to something.

It wasn't long before her efforts made a notable impact. She testified before the state legislature about her life as a foster child, and what it felt like to wonder every day if you were about to lose your foster parents and your home.

As a result of her testimony, policy changes were made. Unless there was a real concern, or reason to remove the children, the state was obligated to respect the relationship more than a diagnosis.

Clearly, having been raised by an ill foster parent, lit a fire under Olivia to protect other foster families from experiencing the fear and stress we had about being taken away. We were all so proud of her.

Chase was a full-fledged attorney now, and working as the county's public defender. Neither Olivia nor I were too excited about his job. Over the years, drug usage had increased exponentially, and the criminals, even in our small town, seemed significantly scarier than when we were young.

Regardless, he was determined to become a judge one day. Whenever we challenged him about his job, usually when he was working on a really scary case, he'd tell us it was a prerequisite to judgeship.

For the most part, we got into a nice routine. Absent Miss Margaret, of course.

We all came to appreciate just how much her life had changed in the past year. Miss Margaret arrived at the house with a slim, elegant woman on her heels. "Children—" Miss Margaret said in her most authoritative voice, "—this is my girlfriend, Emma Ericksen. I've asked her to spend Christmas with us."

My eyebrows met my hairline as I looked over at Olivia and Chase, who both looked as shocked as I was. It took all of five minutes for us to adore Miss Emma Ericksen, though, including when she shyly said she would prefer we just call her Emma.

"Couldn't be much more opposite," Chase whispered when Miss Margaret and Emma went to the kitchen, leaving us in the parlor with the kids.

Emma wasn't someone we'd have paired with the hard-shelled Miss Margaret, but the woman was so sweet, it was hard not to like her. Besides, opposites attracted, right?

Miss Margaret ended up surprising us a few months later, when she announced during a family dinner that she and Emma were getting married. Even though we sort of expected it, the news still shocked us. Who knew after all this time, all of us would have a significant other in our lives?

Looking back, I regretted the time I struggled with Olivia and Chase's relationship. Now, it just seemed to be right. Miss Margaret and Emma were a beautiful couple as well. Both were about the same age, and clearly in love.

I looked over at Allen and he seemed to be able to sense my thoughts. He smiled and winked at me before digging into Miss Margaret's famous Mexican lasagna she'd taught Chase to make. Olivia was still pathetic in the kitchen, but Chase loved to cook, and his lasagna was almost as good as Miss Margaret's.

My heart felt so full at that moment. Everyone I loved the most was right there in the room, and we were all happy. As I looked at my boyfriend, I realized he was most certainly a big part of the equation. I just hoped I'd be able to keep him that way.

TWENTY-EIGHT

ALLEN

MY WORK LIFE CALMED down quickly when a new crop of medical school graduates began their residencies at the hospital. Since it was my second year, I began taking more shifts in the emergency room as part of my training. I'd pretty-much decided I no longer wanted to pursue administration, at least not for a while. Instead, I decided I'd like to work both in pediatrics as well as emergency care. I loved the day-to-day work with the kids, but I much preferred the fast pace of the emergency room. I guessed I was just someone who did best under pressure.

One of the new emergency-room residents, Les, was beginning to show an interest in me. He'd say something about how good-looking residents were these days, or make a comment about how the scrubs I wore matched my eyes. I did my best to discourage his attention, but no matter what I did or said, he wasn't easily put off.

Things came to a head one evening when Gib came by and dropped off food for me while I was working a night shift. I'd been complaining about how the hospital didn't have adequate food for staff, and had woken up late and left my dinner at home.

When Gib walked in, I immediately walked over to him and kissed him as a thank you for bringing me food. He hung out for a moment, talking to some of the ER staff he'd come to know through me.

Les came in just as Gib was preparing to leave and threw his arm around me in a move he'd never done before. Of course, I looked at him like he'd lost his mind, and Gib cocked an eyebrow.

"Gib, this is Doctor Les Townsend," I said, sliding out from under Les's arm. "And Les, this is my *boyfriend*, Gib!"

Les acted shocked and then put on a mad act. "You never told me you had a boyfriend."

Then in a total drama queen move, he stomped out.

Gib looked at me, the cocked eyebrow never leaving his face, and all I could do was shrug. "No idea," I said as I came around the desk to kiss him.

Since the nurses were all watching the events closely, I decided to walk Gib out, so we could have some privacy.

As soon as we were outside, I sighed. "Gib, I've made it clear to him I'm not interested, but he won't leave me alone. I'm going to have to go to a supervisor if he doesn't take the hint soon."

"Well, if he's willing to make a scene like that in front of the nursing staff and even patients, not to mention your boyfriend, I'd say you might need to do that, like, now," Gib said, and reached over to take my hand. It helped to see that he believed me.

I sighed again. "Just as I was beginning to get my feet under me here. You're right, I'll talk to the supervising physician tomorrow."

For the rest of the night, Les acted like a spurned lover. Our shift ended the following morning at seven, and usually, I'd have gone straight home to sleep. Instead, I waited until nine for Dr. Jeffers to come in, so I could speak to him about last night's incident.

When I explained what happened, he sighed. "Les's father is on the board. I won't pretend this isn't going to cause you some trouble, but you were right to come to me. If he's making a scene, especially trying to create issues between you and your boyfriend, we need to nip it in the bud sooner rather than later."

I went home feeling at least somewhat confident my reporting it would help. I'd still have to work with Les, but maybe a discussion with Dr. Jeffers would convince him to leave me the hell alone.

Unfortunately, nothing could be further from what actually happened. Les made a formal complaint against me, saying we'd had an affair while on duty at the hospital, and that I'd forced him into it. There were more lies of sexual harassment, but that was the gist of it.

Of course, things got worse at home. Gib, I think, trusted me for the most part, but the rumors were pretty damning, and Les had made a very convincing argument against me. I came home after the initial allegations surfaced, and told Gib what Les had said.

Gib didn't hide his emotions well at all, and when I said Les had told the hospital I'd pressured him into a physical relationship, Gib cringed. I couldn't read his expression, and I was concerned Gib might be beginning to question my fidelity as well.

As things continued to spiral, I ended up calling Alexi and breaking down. "Alexi, I don't seem to be able to win. I never showed any interest in the lying twink. He wouldn't leave *me* alone! I think this is going to cost me my residency."

Alexi kept silent and let me sob over the phone, before I finally confessed what was really breaking me. "Gib... I think he might believe the allegations."

"No, Allen, he wouldn't. Just give it some time," she said, consoling me as best she could. Mostly, I just needed a friend to confide in. If I lost my residency and my relationship over this idiot, I didn't know what I'd do. I'd put so much energy and heart into both, and they meant everything to me... the hospital and Gib were my life, really.

I ended up being called into a meeting with the disciplinary committee. Les and his father sat across from me with Dr. Jeffers at the head of the conference-room table. As the committee laid out the allegations, it quickly became clear they were siding with Les.

"You will no longer be allowed to work in the emergency department, Doctor McCartney," the committee chair finally said. "If you don't have any contact with Doctor Townsend, he has agreed not to press any formal charges against you."

Something clicked inside me then, and before I could stop myself, I said, "Then I'll be making a formal charge against him. I believe libel is the appropriate term for what's happened here. As you know, my father is the lead surgeon in one of the largest hospital chains in the Northeast, and he will be helping me hire a *team* of attorneys to conduct a thorough investigation, and prove the allegations leveled against me by Doctor Townsend are false."

I was totally bluffing, at least I was at that point. I knew it was very unlikely my father would actually do anything to help me. In fact, it was more likely he'd side with the committee, but they didn't need to know that.

"I've invested a great deal in this residency, and I need the emergency department experience as much as the pediatrics, so if anyone is to be relieved of their position, it should be the one who made up allegations when he couldn't take no for an answer."

I was standing to go when Dr. Jeffers, my one advocate, spoke up. "Do you officially intend to challenge this committee's decision then?"

I took a deep breath, guessing this was going to be the end of my career, and said, "I most certainly do. Who should I have my attorney contact?"

To my surprise, Dr. Jeffers smiled, and said, "Doctor McCartney, if you and Doctor Townsend could step outside, I'd like to have a word with the committee, then

I will happily give you the number for your attorney to contact." Les stared at me, but I refused to even acknowledge his pitiful existence. Instead, I channeled my father's infamous stoicism, because I'd be damned if the lying SOB got a reaction out of me after this fiasco.

As I walked out of the room, I went down the long hallway toward the window, where I knew I'd be able to get mobile phone coverage and called my father. I'd been pulled into this mess, but fuck if I wasn't willing to use anyone at my disposal if it meant keeping myself in the program.

He answered on the second ring, surprising me. Usually, he never answered my calls.

"Hello?"

"Hi, Dad, it's Allen. I need a favor," I said, speaking low so as not to be overheard.

He was quiet for a moment, then asked, "Is this to do with that creep who made false allegations against you?"

I was shocked. I didn't think Alexi would've told him, but maybe she did since this was serious enough to jeopardize my residency. Then again, given my dad had known about my residency interview without a word from me, he could've heard it from someone else.

"Yeah, and thanks for believing me. I may need the number of an attorney. The disciplinary committee seems to be siding with the lying jackass, probably because his father is on the board. I told them I didn't accept their position, and that I'd be having an attorney contact them. I need to conduct my own investigation into all this, Dad."

"That's wise, son. I'll have my personal attorney contact you and you can discuss it with him. And, son, don't worry, I'll cover the expenses. I won't have some arrogant little shit undo your career, especially after you've worked so hard for it."

I was shocked again. Who the hell was it I was talking to? I honestly thought I'd be having to talk my ass off to convince him I was innocent, let alone to help me. I never even considered he'd take my side.

"I've got to go back into the meeting now, but I'll let you know what the outcome is. Oh, and Dad, thanks. I really needed you on this."

"Son, I'm always here for you, even when you don't think I am."

I hung up as Dr. Jeffers came out of the room, and gestured for me and Les to return. I didn't know what I was walking back into, but knowing I had Dad in my corner was reassuring.

"Doctor McCartney, your request for a full investigation has been granted," Dr. Jeffers said. My first response was, why the hell they hadn't done one already, but Dr. Jeffers gave me a meaningful look, and I could tell he was encouraging me not to make waves.

I nodded, hoping the man really did have my back. "Doctor Townsend, as you know, several people we've spoken to contradict your claims, but since we have a no-tolerance policy on sexual harassment, your word was taken over Doctor McCartney. Of course, now that Doctor McCartney has requested a formal investigation, we will be collecting all the evidence regarding your allegation. Is that clear?"

Les's father's face flushed deep red, and I could tell he was ready to blow a gasket. Les, however, looked like he was about to give birth to a very guilty beachball.

Apparently, using his father's connections to try and get what he wanted—in this case, burning me for spurning him—wasn't working out so well after all. Les and I might have looked similar on paper, being residents from wealthy families with influential physician fathers, but I'd never take advantage of my dad's position for my own selfish gains. Even the idea was sickening.

I was sure for other residents under any circumstances, facing the disciplinary committee would be like going up against a giant, particularly since Les's father served on the hospital board. Until now, I'd never considered myself lucky, having a dad in a powerful position. Most of the time, I'd have said the opposite, but I knew for a fact my father's influence had saved me this time.

I also had no doubt that if my colleagues were honest, Les's allegations would be proven false.

In the end, the investigation wasn't necessary. Within a week, Les withdrew his allegations. His father ended up resigning from the board, and Les's residency was discreetly moved to a different medical facility far away from me.

I'd given the rundown of the situation to my dad's attorney when he'd called, and he assured me he would be in contact with the hospital's legal department, to ensure there would be no backlash against me.

A week later, Dr. Jeffers pulled me into his office for a very candid heart-to-heart.

"Allen, can we have an off-the-record discussion?" he asked.

I nodded, concerned about where this was going.

"Things have been tough for you, tougher than they should've been. I didn't realize you were being worked twice as hard as the other residents, and I found out too late to intervene at an appropriate time. Now, you've been subjected to this mess with Les Townsend."

He stared at me for a long moment, clearly debating what he was about to say. Finally, his face showed resolve, before he said, "I probably shouldn't be this candid with you, especially since your terrifying attorney contacted us, but if it comes back to bite me in the ass, so be it. You're one of the most dedicated, hardworking residents I've ever had the privilege to work with. You're respectful to your coworkers, colleagues, and supervisors, and you're a sponge with information. You also handled that Les issue like a professional. Most other residents would've bowed under the pressure. I can't officially say good job, but unofficially, you did a good job!" He smiled at me then.

I nodded, but the knot in my stomach had not loosened.

"Now the disciplinary committee has heard your side of things, plus the damning evidence we found against your accuser, I've told them you will be working directly under my supervision from this point forward. It'll be unusual, and under normal circumstances, I think I'd have been overruled, but again that attorney you have is scary." He chuckled, before he continued, "I can't promise you don't still have an uphill battle here. The fact is, you came into a program that would normally only be given to graduates of this university. Time and again, you've shown yourself as the exceptional physician you are. Though I think things will be easier with me standing guard, it'll also cause some resentment. I can't really fix that, but I can keep it from coming back to bite you in the ass again."

I took a long deep breath. I hadn't known what the outcome of today's discussion would be, but I was overcome with relief, not to mention excited about working for Dr. Jeffers... even if my excitement was tempered by the events that'd led to it.

"I don't mind the pressure," I said. "To be honest, I think it's helped me be a better resident, but I would like it if I wasn't fighting to survive here. One allegation, a clearly false one, and I almost lost the emergency medicine side of my residency. I don't like to accept help. In fact, normally, I'd argue with you about it, but I think if you don't step in, I may not survive here much longer."

The older man nodded sadly. "I'd hoped it would be different, but unfortunately, as with any teaching hospital, things can be cliquish. Keep your chin up, though, and keep up the good work. Everyone here knows what kind of physician you are."

I left feeling better, since, apparently, things were finally looking up at work. I went home excited to share the positive news with Gib.

Twenty-Nine

Gib

I T WAS UNFAIR. I knew it was unfair, yet I couldn't help it. Reminiscent of how difficult it had been for me to deal with Olivia and Chase, that's how hard it was for me to convince myself the allegations levied against Allen had no merit.

I think the real issue was that I'd seen Allen go through men like they were Kleenex. Use them, then toss them to the side. I'd worried that he'd eventually tire of me, and to be honest, the unreasonable side of my brain kept telling me that was what had happened here.

Of course, the reasonable side assured me the ugly little man who'd flamed out on him when he saw us kissing was anything but Allen's type. He'd been consistent with his men. They were all at least six feet tall and muscular, most had been much more muscular than me, and I'd never seen him with a twinky-type guy. On more than one occasion, I'd seen him squash like a bug under a flyswatter anyone who made a move, but didn't fit his type. So, no, the twink wasn't telling the truth. I just needed to convince my heart.

I did what I could to support him while he was going through the disciplinary process and investigation. I made it a point to put my whacked-out feelings aside, so I could focus on being the supportive boyfriend. The night he told me how the twink had been called out on his lies and moved to a different hospital, I felt something change in me, something I just didn't have the power to ignore.

I didn't believe Allen cheated on me, but I did think it was just a matter of time. I tried to ignore the feelings, tried to rationalize them, or push them away, but as the months went by, I became more and more distressed. I could feel myself pulling away, shutting him out, but I felt powerless to stop it.

Allen flew home to New York for Thanksgiving, but I refused to go with him. While he was gone, I moved out of the house and into an apartment a few miles closer to the clinic. I was waiting for him when he got home.

He must've known something was up, because he was on the verge of tears before even realizing I'd packed up my stuff and moved out.

"Allen, I'm so sorry. I just can't do this any longer. And, before you ask, it's nothing you've done or not done. I'm just not emotionally together enough to handle being in this kind of relationship," I said, desperately wanting him to understand.

"So, you're going with the *it's me, not you* conversation?" he asked. I could see he was beginning to get angry, and I knew I deserved it.

"It's the truth."

"Yeah, it is. I've done everything to make this work, Gib. I love you, I've been completely honest with you, but you've kept me at arm's length. It *is* you, *not* me," he said. I could tell he was about to cry, and I wanted to go to him, apologize, tell him I was sorry... but as he got up and walked toward the bedroom, I didn't do any of that.

I honestly didn't know what to do, so I sat in the living room waiting for him to come back. When he didn't, I put my key on the coffee table. "Allen, I'm going," I called out.

When he didn't respond, I left. Was that really it? As I drove to my tiny studio apartment, I felt my heart break into a thousand pieces.

The month between Thanksgiving and Christmas was horrible. When my family gathered together on Christmas Eve, Chrissy was clearly upset that I hadn't brought Allen with me. Even the twins asked several times where Uncle Allen was, and each time it sent me into an emotional spiral.

When Olivia finally asked, I was barely able to croak out that we'd broken up, before hurrying from the room on the verge of tears. I didn't want the girls to see their uncle cry, let alone break down in front of the adults.

To my surprise, Olivia didn't follow me. I figured it was Chase who intervened to ensure I had some space.

Even watching my nieces squealing in delight while opening their Christmas gifts wasn't enough to lift my spirits. I cried through the entire holiday, and was seriously depressed when I returned to work. Before, the world had color, and now without Allen, it was gray and bleak.

I had seriously fucked things up. I'd been so afraid of Allen breaking my heart that I broke it myself before he had the chance. He was right. I was the problem. That didn't mean I had a clue how to fix it.

THIRTY

ALLEN

I COULDN'T STOP CRYING. I managed to keep my emotions in check at work, but if I took a break, even for a quick lunch, I ended up bawling my eyes out. I flew to New York to spend Christmas with my mom after she told me she'd be back in the States for the holiday.

I was sure it wasn't the merry Christmas my mom had been hoping to spend with me, but she went into full Mom mode the minute she saw me. I let her console me, and was surprised that even Dad had been somewhat supportive. For the most part, though, I could tell he didn't really want to be involved with my love life, or lack thereof.

When I got back to the hospital, the depression just deepened, so I called Fiona and Alexi and asked them to visit. I'd have gone to them, of course, but I'd just taken all the time off I could.

They arrived the following weekend, and ended up helping me process what'd happened.

"He did wrong, dumping you with no clear explanation," Fiona said, and Alexi agreed.

They were ready to go into trashing Gib mode, but I found myself defending him. "No, he had a reason. It's because of what Les said. He thinks I'm still a slut."

"No," Alexi said, "Gib is smarter than that, there's got to be more."

"He's probably afraid," Fiona said. "Gib is sort of good at pushing people away."

I opened my mouth to defend him again and made myself stop. *Fuck that. How is it he can break my heart, and I still want to defend him?*

Even though they didn't tell me, I knew they were headed to Gib's after I left for work on Monday. Secretly, I hoped they would talk some sense into him. Did that just make me even more pathetic? He'd hurt me so much, and I still hoped to get him back.

Time didn't heal all wounds... it didn't heal a fucking thing. Like a massive injury, it would eventually scar over, and the pain might or might not stop. In my case, it didn't.

Alexi and Fiona left on Tuesday, both having to get back to their jobs. They'd helped. Not fixed it. I wasn't sure what would fix how shattered I felt, but it'd helped.

In the end, the person who helped the most was my mom. She called me one Friday while I was on break.

"Hello, Allen. I'm in Nashville."

"Wow, okay," I said, wondering if she was here for work, or this was a ruse to see me.

"So, I want to do dinner. When are you free next?" she asked.

I had the next day off, so I invited her to my house and fixed spaghetti and meatballs. It was something I used to do when I was a teenager, and she was working late. "So, why don't you stay here while you're in town?" I asked over dinner. I knew how much she disliked staying in a hotel she was having to beat back into shape, not to mention I could use the company.

"Honey, no one wants their mother living with them," she said.

I laughed. "Mom, I'm hardly ever here, and you're wrong, I miss you."

She moved in after that and I loved having her there, as much for her company as not having to come home to an empty house.

When I'd seen her at Christmas, I'd told her Gib had moved out, so one evening when I was particularly weepy, I'd confided in her about everything that happened.

"Allen, honey, I'm so sorry. Gib seemed like a nice kid, but from my conversations with his foster mom, he definitely struggles with his relationships with others. It's not just you, baby."

I was surprised. First, to learn that Mom was still in contact with Miss Margaret. Second, I was shocked that she and Mom had discussed Gib.

"Mom, he just doesn't trust me."

"And why would you say that?" she asked. She didn't sound accusing, but Mom didn't beat around the bush either.

"'Cause, when we first met, I was a slut. I stopped all that after developing feelings for him, and he knows it. He changed when I was accused of sexual harassment. It's like he shut down and I was never able to get him to talk about it." The tears fell again. "And, Mom, I can't be with someone who doesn't trust me. I was faithful to him even before we became boyfriends, so it's unfair that he's labeled me this way."

"It is, sweetheart, it is," she said, rubbing my back in comfort.

We sat in silence for a moment as I wiped away my tears and took some deep breaths to calm myself. "I'm so tired of crying, let's go out," I said, shocking her.

"Where do you wanna go?" she asked.

"Well, let's go do touristy stuff. Wanna go see the Grand Ole Opry?"

She chuckled. "I thought you didn't like country music?"

"It's growing on me, but mostly I hate being this weepy mess. I can't fix what's going on with Gib and me, but I can get back on my damned feet, even if it still hurts."

"That's my boy," she said, and we spent the rest of the day touring the sights of Nashville.

THIRTY-ONE

GIB

"HI, GIB," ALEXI SAID when I answered my phone. "So, Fiona and I are in town. Do you have time to meet?"

Of course, I agreed to meet my friends, although I cringed since I expected quite a shit show was about to come my way.

I'd been wrong, though. The two women were supportive, if not a bit miffed at me. They could see how emotional I was about it all, so they didn't push.

"Allen's upset, of course," Fiona said, and Alexi nodded as we sat in the small diner next to my clinic. "But, we're your friend too, Gib. I just hope you know what you're doing."

I nodded, but didn't comment. There was nothing to say anyway, because I *didn't* know what the fuck I was doing... except reacting the only way I knew how.

Before they left, Fiona asked, "Are you sure you're willing to throw your relationship with Allen away?"

I shook my head. "No, ultimately I want him in my life. That's why I had to pull away. If I'd stayed, I'd have ended up destroying us completely."

Fiona looked at me sadly. Her expression said it all, *maybe I already had*.

I threw myself into work and family after that, not allowing any emotions about Allen to seep into my life. Winter quickly bled into spring, and before I knew it, Alexi had phoned to ask if I would consider joining them at the Martha's Vineyard house again. Of course, I declined. I was the reason Allen and I were in this heartbroken mess, and he had every right to go and have a good time with his friends. *Our* friends.

It'd been almost five months since I'd moved out of Allen's house, and we still hadn't talked. There wasn't a day went by that I didn't think of him, though. How was he doing? What was his residency like now the head of the teaching department was directly supervising him? Did he miss me as much as I missed him? Would he ever speak to me again?

Everything in me hungered to have him back in my arms, but the lingering doubt kept me at bay.

During the week my friends were gathered on Martha's Vineyard, I was an emotional wreck. Brenda, our nurse practitioner, thought I was sick and sent me home on Wednesday, telling me not to come back until I'd gotten some rest. That was actually the opposite of what I needed. Being home alone with nothing but my thoughts just made things worse. So, naturally, I ended up spending the rest of the week with Olivia, Chase, and the girls.

By Saturday, Olivia had had enough, and sat me down in what used to be the formal living room, but was now a corral for the twins. "Spill," she said.

"What?" I asked, playing innocent.

"You're moping around here like you did when that stray dog you fell in love with was adopted by the family from Memphis."

I hadn't thought of that moment in a long time, but she was right. That's exactly how I felt. Alone, dejected, and without the one thing I wanted more than anything else.

"Olivia, it's just me getting over Allen."

"And why?"

"Why what?" I asked, confused about what she meant.

"Why are you getting over Allen?"

Leave it to Olivia to shock me into silence. It took me a moment to remember the excuses I'd given myself about why I was right to break up with him.

"He's not the kind of guy who settles down with just one man," I said. Of course, I didn't really believe that any longer, but I figured it was the one excuse that would appease my sister. Unfortunately, I was wrong.

She leaned in close, so only I could hear, and said, "Bullshit, Gib. That man never cheated on you, and we both know it."

She had me on that one. "Olivia, he'll be going back to New York in a couple years. It's better to pull the tape off now before I get too attached."

She stood up and began throwing toys into different toy boxes around the room. "You are totally full of fucking shit!" she said angrily, although still in a quiet voice, since the soon-to-be three-year-olds, as well as the soon-to-be kindergartener, would pick up on the words like a nail to a magnet.

"You're pushing him away, just like you pushed Chase and me away, and why? Just 'cause you can't deal with things not being exactly how you think they should be. Damn, brother, I'm so frustrated with you. Allen adores you, or at least he did. *We* fucking adored you." She threw a doll into the toy chest and turned to go. "You need to get your head on straight, and you need to do it before you end up losing the love of your life, and frankly, brother, I don't give a damn whether this conversation pisses you off or not."

I stared at her retreating back as she left the room. I could hear her tending to the girls in the main living room and decided to take my leave. I walked out the front door and headed for the old barn hill. It was the best place for thinking, and Olivia had given me a lot to think about.

I'd only been there a couple minutes when Chase showed up. I almost laughed. This was so much like our childhood. Olivia seldom gave me what for any longer, but when she did, Chase usually came to comfort me. We'd both been on the receiving end of her temper, and although we almost always deserved it, it still stung.

Chase sat next to me, and began pulling strands of grass just like I'd been doing before he showed up. We sat like that for at least fifteen minutes, before he finally said, "You know she's right."

I looked at him, shrugged, then went back to pulling up grass.

"I love you, Gib. You're one of the most important people in my life, but, brother, you're a stubborn wall of brick sometimes too. Tell me the truth, why did you push Allen away?"

I leaned back against the cold stone wall and stared up at the sky for several long minutes.

"I'm not enough," I finally said.

He didn't respond right away. It was a feeling we'd both talked about over the years. I hadn't been enough to save my parents, Mr. Simmons, or Mrs. Simmons. I knew kids internalized things, and I had internalized all the losses in my life. Knowing that didn't ease the hurt, though.

"You and I both know that's all the shitty foster-kid stuff, but I'll give that to you for a minute. How could you be enough? What would you have to be like to be enough?" he asked.

I shrugged. To be honest, I couldn't answer that question now, any more than I could've answered it when I was a kid.

He let me struggle with the question for a moment, before he finally said, "You will never convince that kid inside you that you aren't a loser who caused his family to disappear. The fear of losing Mrs. Simmons just made it worse for all three of us." He paused as if considering his next words, then chuckled. "It was good for getting us to pursue degrees and high-end jobs. All three of us are ridiculously ambitious, but, Gib, eventually you gotta tell that little boy inside you to shut up and get a life."

We sat silently for another long stretch, before he finally sighed. "You were wrong in how you treated Olivia and me. It hurt, hell, it still hurts. I understand why you did it, but, dude, I doubt it'll ever stop hurting. Seeing you do it to another person you love is almost more than either of us can bear."

He stood up and pulled me with him. "Listen, if you don't love this guy, fine, let it go, be done with it, but if, as I suspect, you do love him, then stop being a scared little kid, and tell him how you feel. Let him help you work through all these feelings of inadequacy."

He embraced me then and held me while I cried it out. Chase was shorter than Allen, but he was stout as a bull. It didn't happen often, but when things got bad, there was nothing like having the strength of my brother's arms around me to work through the tough times.

When I finally managed to stem the tide of my tears, he pulled back and smiled. "If you ever need your ass kicked again, I highly recommend you come to me first, so we can work it out before Olivia gets ahold of it." He sighed long and sad, before saying, "You know she's gonna be pissed for weeks now, and you'll be off doing the doctor thing while the girls and I have to deal with her badass attitude."

I chuckled. "Lucky for you, I'm gonna go eat crow. She loves it when you admit she's right. I'm guessing things will be so good for you after this, you and the girls will owe me at least a round of pizza!"

Chase smiled. "That's true, and if you clean this up before you leave, I'll be more than happy to foot the cost of that pizza."

Olivia had given me another earful after we put the girls to bed, and she could speak without having to whisper. Of course, she just got angrier when Chase and I glanced at each other and chuckled.

"Oh my god, I'm gonna kill you both!" she said, exasperated.

"Breathe, Olivia, you're right. I've been an idiot. I told Chase earlier I was going to confess that to you."

She looked at me skeptically. In our childhood, she and I had gone round and round for days when we'd disagreed about something like this. It was rare for me to just admit she was right, and I could tell she was struggling with how to handle it.

I made the mistake of looking at Chase again, because this time when we burst into laughter, Olivia hit me hard on the arm.

"Ouch! Dang, Olivia, that hurts."

"It was meant to, you jackass!"

She collapsed on the sofa they'd bought when Miss Margaret moved all the fancy furniture out of the house and stored it God only knew where. Most of it was original to the house and a work of art, but it was some of the most uncomfortable stuff to sit on, and was in no way made for young kids.

I sat across from her, and said, "I'm going to clean things up with Allen, but apparently, I still need to clean things up with you two as well."

When Chase sat next to her, she leaned into him, and I knew it was time to make things right.

"As Chase said to me earlier, I'm still that same little foster kid who came to this house all those years ago, scared and mistrusting. It took a long time for me to let Mr. or Mrs. Simmons anywhere near me. I cried every night those first few weeks." I paused as the memory swept over me. I'd never told them about the time before they came to live there.

"When they told me you two were moving in, I was honestly scared to death. I'd been in another foster home where they'd taken in a baby, then within a few weeks, I'd been moved. I was convinced the two of you were going to be the end of my life here. I hadn't been prepared to find two people I would love as much as I love y'all. Unfortunately, my entire life I've been waiting to lose you, Mrs. Simmons, this home, even Miss Margaret.

"I spent the whole time at Harvard waiting for them to tell me I had to go home, that I was an imposter or something," I said, wiping at the tears. "Allen, Fiona, and Alexi, they were a surprise to me like y'all were. I wasn't prepared to love them, but that's basically what happened. I know I screwed up when you two became a couple, and missed out on Chrissy's early years as a result, but I just wasn't emotionally capable of dealing with the perceived loss of you as my sister and brother.

It took all that time for me to make sense of it, and of course, a good talking to by Miss Margaret about what I was losing by dragging my feet."

"Now you're doing the same thing to Allen," Olivia accused again. My sister wasn't one to forgive what she considered silliness.

I nodded. "Yeah, now I've done the same thing to Allen. Although, in my defense, until you yelled at me, I didn't quite understand that's what I was doing."

Olivia huffed out a breath. "I should've yelled at you months ago. Both Chase and I saw it clear as day. Even Miss Margaret agrees. You need to put this right before you lose him, Gib."

She turned to Chase and sighed. "I know I said I'd stay out of it, but damn, if we don't say something, he'll march through his miserable life alone, forcing us to watch him throw a chance with a perfectly delightful man out the window. I've seen enough of that to last a lifetime."

Chase just chuckled quietly. "Baby, I knew you wouldn't stay out of it for long. Miss Margaret and I have been quite impressed you kept it together this long."

She elbowed him in the ribs, making him wince. "Gib, fix this and do it *now* before it's too late."

"I will, sister. I will," I said, and she nodded.

She looked up the stairs to where the girls were asleep, then said, "I really need a drink. Chase, you've got kid duty. I'm going to pull down the Fireball, and Gib and I are going to drink what's left of the bottle."

"Yes, dear," was all Chase said, because, bless his heart, he knew when we were at our wits' end. Luckily, the alcohol would mitigate some of the stress. When we were kids, it often ended up being much louder as we worked through our emotional turmoil.

Later that night, after Olivia drank three-times-more whisky than me, I picked up my phone and called Fiona, knowing my night-owl friends would still be awake despite the time difference. That, and they were on vacation together, after all. She picked up on the first ring, and I could tell she was putting me on speaker.

"Hey, is everyone there?"

"Yep, you've got us all," Alexi said.

"Good, 'cause I've never been this freaking sad... well, that's not quite true. Allen, I was sadder in December when I screwed things up, but I've been miserable beyond words this week. I screwed up with all of you, especially you, Allen."

The group was silent, which I expected. "Okay, I love you all. I miss you and..." I was wiping away the tears and getting choked up, so I decided to cut my call short. "Okay, so I'll talk later," I said, hanging up before anyone had a chance to respond.

Alone in the living room, I lay down on the sofa, and bawled like a freaking baby. Alexi called me back a couple times, but I was too distraught to answer. I'd try to call her back later when I had enough of my shit together.

I woke up on the couch sometime later to Alexi calling again, and I answered, although my stomach felt like it'd been filled with concrete.

"Hey," she said.

"Hi," I answered back, too shy really to say much else.

"So, I'm sorry about that call."

"Yeah, me too. I didn't mean to be a drama queen."

She laughed. "My god, Gib, you're not a drama queen. You're fucked up, but you're not a drama queen."

"Yeah," I agreed. "So, how's Allen?"

"You need to ask him that yourself. He's hurt, but you already know that."

I sat silently before finally asking, "Alexi, I'm not sure how. Should I try to see him?"

"I don't know, Gib," she said sadly. "I think he wants to see you, but it probably should be on his terms. If you don't hear from him in the next couple of weeks, though, you should reach out to him. See if he'll consider meeting to talk things out."

"Thanks, Alexi."

I didn't have it in me to ask if they had fun at the Vineyard. The truth was, I didn't really want to know. It broke my heart that I hadn't gone with them. Now it'd be a whole year before I had a chance to spend time with them again.

Olivia found me milling around the kitchen a little while later. "You coming to church with us tomorrow?" she asked, and I cringed.

"Um, no, thank you. Church is not on my radar at the moment."

"You know you probably should go, but if it wasn't for the girls, I'd probably play hooky myself."

I smiled. Olivia had never been big on going to church. In fact, she flat-out refused to go when she was in college, but nowadays, she was all but the quintessential church lady.

"I think I'll sleep in tomorrow. I've agreed to go in at seven every day this coming week to get the patient load down a little. It just seems like we're getting more and more slammed as the year goes on."

"Well, I envy your morning sleep in, but I won't interfere with it, although I'd like to do the Mrs. Simmons thing, and bang pots and pans down here until you wake up."

I chuckled at the memory. The woman had been a saint in most ways, but she couldn't stand us sleeping late in the mornings. Her slamming pots and pans was a sure-fire way to get us out of bed long before normal teenagers.

I was shocked out of sleep the next morning when Olivia knocked on my door, then burst in saying Allen was here, and waiting for me downstairs. I dashed out of bed and rushed into the bathroom, tossing cold water on my face hoping it'd help wake me up. I quickly brushed my teeth too, then rushed out of the room and down the stairs, where I heard him talking to my nieces.

THIRTY-TWO

ALLEN

WE HAD BEEN LESS than fun as a group this past week. No matter how you shook things out, Gib's absence was palpable. The fact he called on Friday night, the night before the trip was over, should've ended in celebration and teasing. Instead, it ended with him breaking down on the phone, then refusing to answer when we called him back.

I knew the girls hadn't responded to him to give me the chance to do so. Just the day before, Alexi had nailed me, asking, "If you still want him, why aren't you fighting for him?"

My pride. That was the only answer I had, and fuck if I was going to admit that.

She'd been right, though. I'd fought for what I wanted all my life. My dad had been a jackass and I'd turned to my mom, who gave me everything I needed to be a strong, emotionally stable man.

When Dad put unrealistic expectations on me, I'd met and exceeded them. I'd gone to Harvard, not because I had to or it was expected of me, but because it was what I wanted.

Now, I'd proven the same things time and again in a contentious residency. I had what it took to fight for myself, so why had I let Gib pull away without a fight?

The answer was simple. My heart was broken. After Alexi badgered me a little longer, I said, "I want *him* to fight for *me*."

"But, what if he can't fight for you? What if his heart isn't strong enough?" Alexi asked.

"What do you mean?"

"You're a freaking pediatrician, Allen. You've surely worked with abused and neglected children. Would you expect those children to be able to work through complex emotional issues?"

"Not without help," I admitted.

"Well, Gib's one of those kids. I mean, he's smart, a talented doctor, a great friend, and all that, but he's still that kid."

Of course, that phone call all but proved what Alexi had said. He was in an intense amount of pain.

As I flew back to Tennessee, I resolved to confront the man, and force him to at least admit why he was pushing me away. I loved him enough to forgive him for not being able to be my lover, but I'd be damned if I let him throw away our friendship.

I flew into Nashville in the wee hours of Sunday morning. Fiona and Alexi had Gib's address, so I drove straight to his apartment, hoping he'd be home since it was still so early. When I knocked repeatedly and no one answered, I knew immediately where he was. He was back home with his siblings.

I didn't even blink. I got back in my car and drove to the big old Victorian home. When I knocked, Chrissy answered the door in her Sunday outfit, and immediately leaped into my arms. "Uncle Allen's here!" she yelled into the house.

She turned back to me then, looking up with eyes wide. "I've missed you, Uncle Allen," she said sadly. "Why have you been gone so long?"

Leave it to a child to cut to the quick. "'Cause, I've been being silly. How have you been?" I asked as I saw Olivia and Chase come into the hallway.

"I'm good. Wanna see me ride my bike? I have training wheels," she said proudly.

"Of course, I do," I said, but Olivia stopped her before she could dash outside in her stark white knee socks without shoes on.

"We'll show Allen when we get back from church," she told Chrissy, then shooed her back into the house, while she all but pulled me into the hallway.

"Is, um... Gib here?" I asked, feeling very shy all of a sudden.

"The sulking mess is still in bed. You can sit in the kitchen with the girls while Chase finishes feeding them. I'll go get His Majesty up, and let him know you're here."

I could hear the agitation in Olivia's voice, and had to all but bite my tongue to keep from smiling. Olivia was in every way what you'd think an older sister would be like. The fact that she was the same age as Gib did nothing to lessen her power as the big sister.

I laughed at the mess the girls had made while their poor father was trying to feed them. Mostly, they were playing with the food, getting it in their hair and all over the floor. Within seconds, Gib was standing in the kitchen. The cutoff sweats and ratty t-shirt he wore as pajamas while visiting his family were so familiar to me I felt my heart quiver.

"Hi," I said, just as Ruby pelted me with some of her eggs.

The serious expression he wore melted at the sight of his niece. I reached over, taking the paper towel her father was handing me, and wiped the remains of the egg off my shirt, then I reached down and picked the egg off the floor.

Olivia came in behind Gib, saying it was time to bathe the twins. She and Chase quickly dashed away up the stairs, each with a baby in their arms, and with Chrissy on their heels.

I went over and sat at the small table I'd seen them sometimes use for the girls. "Can we talk?" I asked when he sat in the chair across from me.

"Yeah, I'd like that," he replied, and I thought for the first time in months, things might still have a chance of being okay.

Thirty-Three

Gib

I walked into the kitchen just in time to see Ruby sling a spoonful of eggs onto Allen's shirt. I almost chuckled, because I'd been hit by Ruby's offending food toss more than once this weekend alone.

Within moments, Olivia and Chase had each grabbed a toddler, and were rushing up the stairs with Chrissy in tow to give us some peace. I almost wanted to laugh at my matchmaking sister and brother, but the only thing I could concentrate on was the man in front of me. Allen was here and willing to give me a chance to talk. I might not be big on church, but I was sure praying to God that it meant I might have a chance to put things right.

As we sat at the barely used small table in the kitchen, my mind racing with how to approach this, I had to work not to let the waterworks start again. My god, when had I become such a crybaby?

"Listen, Allen, if you don't mind, I have a lot I'd like to say. Stuff I didn't really understand until recently."

When he nodded, I launched into explaining how it'd felt growing up, even sharing with him the same story I'd told Olivia and Chase the night before. When I finally finished, he stared at me, and said, "I should've gone for psychiatry."

"What?" I asked, a smile forming on my face. "You think you could diagnose me as something?"

"No, I need self-diagnosis."

When I looked at him funny, he chuckled. "Gib, I love you and as crazy as all this has been, all I want is you back in my life, and before you start thinking how codependent I am, no, you'll have to work through all this stuff, and promise me you won't run away when things get scary or confusing, or whatever. I'm not sure I can go through all this again. My heart is too broken from the past few months, but..." He paused to take my hand in his. "...I need you, Gib. Like I need water or food... or air."

I nodded. "Yeah, I need you too. It felt like I was going to break in half since I left."

"Good," he said, and stood up. "'Cause, that's how it's felt to me too, and damn, I think you should've been in as much pain as me."

Just then, Olivia and Chase came downstairs with the little ones. Olivia must've heard the conversation, because she came into the kitchen, and said, "No, my brother needed to hurt more than you, 'cause he's..." She looked at the girls, automatically tempering whatever it was she was about to say, then gave Allen a wink. "...a shmuck."

I hugged the girls, then Olivia and Chase as they all prepared to leave for church, and told them I was going to spend the day with Allen. I dashed up to my old bedroom, the one room in the house that had stayed the same after Miss Margaret moved out, and packed my things. I had the rest of today to spend with Allen, and if there was even half a chance that we'd work through some of this, it would be more than worth it.

THIRTY-FOUR

ALLEN

WE ENDED UP DRIVING to a state archeological site that was split by a scenic little river. Much of the area had secluded benches allowing us to chat in private.

I'd discovered the place in the spring when I was looking for outdoor areas to hike, or if I'm honest, to wallow in self-pity. It was one of my favorites, because since I'd started coming here, I'd seen less than a handful of people, and never anyone on a Sunday.

There was more for us to discuss, but being alone with Gib in this secluded spot, words could wait. So, as the warm early summer sun shone down on us, I cuddled into his arms once again, and just enjoyed the feeling of having him back.

Finally, I turned to him, and said, "I've never been so hurt, Gib. Even my dad, who was mostly an ass when I was growing up, never caused me pain like you did when you rejected me."

He nodded, sadness permeating his features. "I know I hurt you. My heart breaks when I think about it, Allen."

I sighed and leaned back into him. "When did you realize you'd fucked up?"

I chuckled. "I think I knew the day I drove away the last time we spoke, but my insides were so messed up, I couldn't make sense of them. Then Olivia, well, she did what she tends to do when I'm being an idiot, and slapped me around with her words."

"And that helped?"

"Believe it or not, it did, mostly 'cause I already knew she was right. I'd been moping around so bad at work, Brenda thought I was sick and forced me to go home, afraid I was going to give the patients something. But, since I couldn't handle being alone, I ended up going to Chase and Olivia's, and, well, that's when she nailed me."

"Remind me to send her flowers," I said.

"No way, she's already full of herself, 'cause I've admitted I was wrong. If you send her flowers, she'll be impossible to be around."

"I think it's appropriate, don't you?" I asked honestly.

"Yeah, maybe." Gib pulled back and turned me to look at him. "Are you sure you're okay with this? I mean, it's been months since..."

"Since you broke my heart."

"Yeah, since then."

"I don't know, Gib. No, I don't think it's going to go back to how it was before. You'd never intentionally done anything to hurt me before. I'm going to have to have some time, and maybe even some of that therapy we talked about earlier to forgive you, but I really do wanna try. I don't want to live without you."

Gib regarded me for a long moment, then sighed. "I need to come clean, Allen. I got really worked up over that idiot, Les. I think things were mounting up before then, but I guess I was just waiting for you to have had enough of me and kick me to the curb."

I had to push the anger down. "I didn't do anything with that ugly toad of a man," I said, and Gib laughed.

"No, baby, I know you didn't and wouldn't. It didn't have anything to do with him. It was me processing my fear of being left alone. Les was the last straw that caused me to break down. It's still hard for me not to want to run away and hide. I don't want to cause you any more pain, but you deserve to know about the storm raging inside me. I keep having to convince myself you're not going to find some man more deserving than me. Even now, that small voice in the back of my mind is telling me it's a possibility. What's even scarier is that you'll finish your residency, then be off to live in New York or Florida, or some ocean paradise, and I'll have to choose to leave my family or lose you again."

"So, what?" I asked. "You get rid of me before you lose me?"

Gib sighed. "Yeah. I think that's exactly what I was doing."

I reached up and pulled the man's face down to mine before kissing him. "I can't promise that we are forever, although I'd totally commit to that if you asked. I do know I love you, and no other man has ever come close to enticing me away. Not that I don't look at a sexy man who walks in front of me, I still have eyes after all, but you're the only man I want to touch and be touched by. Somewhere inside you, you have to know that's true."

Gib nodded, before saying, "I guess since that's how I feel about you too, it's easy to admit."

"As far as what happens after our residencies, I don't know. I like it here. I'm not sure I want to stay in the wasp's nest I'm in at the moment, but I could see myself working as a pediatrician here in Nashville. I mean, I fully intend to travel, and take plenty of time off once my residency is done, maybe even go back to Greece and sail the islands with my dad and brother, but, baby, I want you to go with me. I wanted you with me this past week."

"So, you really would consider staying here?"

I looked around. "Um, have you looked at this place? It's one of the most beautiful parts of the world I've ever been in. If you go east of the city, it gets even more picturesque. Not only that, I like being needed. Every day, I feel like I've helped make some kid... some family's life better. There aren't many things that feel that good, ya know?"

Gib smiled. "Yeah, I know."

That night, I followed Gib back to his apartment, and we spent the night cuddled in each other's arms. My final thoughts before falling into a blissful sleep left me feeling more hopeful about the future than I had been in nearly a year. *This is exactly how things are supposed to be, and God help me, we'll work this out if it's the last thing I do.*

⚜

"Mom, for the last time, no, I'm not making a mistake. Gib is sorry for how things were left."

She looked at me skeptically, but didn't push the issue any further. Mom wasn't Gib's greatest fan at the moment. Sure, she understood the stuff about his childhood and fear of losing people. She'd even become friends with his foster mom, Miss Margaret, but that wasn't enough for her to let him off the hook.

"Are you going to be able to be nice to him tonight, or should I cancel things? Or, better yet, just go somewhere with him alone?"

"Do what you think is best, sweetheart. Just know that you can try to hide that boy from me all you want, Allen darling, but I will have my say one way or the other. If not tonight, I'll go to his apartment myself. Or better yet, I'll get Margaret to go with me."

I sighed. She wasn't kidding. She'd totally do that. At least, if I was with her, I could possibly block some of the tidal wave headed his way.

"Mom, at least promise you'll let him explain, and not just lay into him for thirty minutes."

She narrowed her eyes at me, which almost made me laugh. The woman was a born lecturer. Her employees quivered in their shoes when she was on a rant, and having been the target of more than one of them myself, I knew how intense they could be.

Despite that, she'd argue that she never lectured. "I will have my say and that will be that, but no, I won't temper it to be nice. The boy hurt you, and since I know you probably didn't hold him accountable, I will. You'll thank me later, Allen."

Yeah, if I was sleeping alone in my bed missing Gib again, I was sure I'd be thanking her.

Satisfied with having the last word, she went to her bedroom. All these months later, she was still living in my house. Her excuse was that Grandpa had followed her advice, and was slowly liquidating the company's European assets. I was almost sure Mom's moving in wasn't really about business. She wanted to keep her eye on me to make sure I was okay. In her defense, I was a massive puddle of despair for several months after the breakup. I really had needed her.

However, now things were improving, I'd love her to find her own place again.

I sighed at that thought, then had to shake off my guilt. I knew Mom was up in the air. She'd sold her New York brownstone after I'd started medical school. She could move back into the apartment in the Manhattan hotel my grandparents lived in, but she said she hated living in the hotels the family owned. So, here she was, living with me.

Of course, I was rarely home, but since I had a boyfriend again, I would have preferred not to have to deal with my mom on the rare occasions I got to see him.

I'd told her we were back together the week after I'd gotten back from Martha's Vineyard. She had been silent for so long, I thought it would just blow over. Well, not really. Mom wasn't one to let things blow over. Instead, she'd waited until now to say she wanted me to invite him over for dinner.

I'd hesitantly done so, then when the date was set, she'd told me exactly what she intended to say to him. I'd begged her to back down, and she frankly refused. I would've prevented the meeting, but in the long run, I wanted Mom to like Gib the same way she had before the breakup. For that to ever happen, I'd have to let her have her say.

Gib arrived right on time, walked in, and sat across from Mom, while I grabbed a bottle of wine, opening it and letting it breathe before pouring us all a glass.

It was awkward for a moment, before Mom finally said, "Gib, I wanted to have my say, and I'm not one to mince words. You broke Allen's heart. I know relationships can be tricky, but people deserve the chance to work through their problems together, not have someone run off when it gets hard."

She stood up, went to the table where the wine sat, and poured herself a full glass. "I loved Allen's father, more than I've loved any other man before or since, but when things got difficult, he ran off with another woman. Now, I know that's not what you did, but it did look an awful lot like it."

She looked over at me, and sighed as she sat back down. "I'm Allen's mother, and of course, seeing your baby hurt, that's like the worst pain for a parent. I don't mind you knowing how miserable he was these past several months. In fact, I've never seen him so distraught."

"Mom," I said under my breath, frustrated that she was having to go there, but even more embarrassed that she was telling him how utterly destroyed I'd been.

I knew she'd heard me, but she fixed her attention on Gib, and took a long drink of wine. "Gib, I like you. I don't want to right now, but damn, I still do. But, the next time you have some kind of emotional breakdown, you need to get a therapist or something. You don't run off breaking everyone's heart as you go."

She stood back up, clearly about to head into the kitchen. As uncomfortable as she'd made me, I was proud of her. She was letting it go a lot faster than she usually did when things upset her.

"Miss Catherine," Gib said, and I almost moaned. *Please, Gib, let her go, let her go.* To my utter horror, though, he didn't. "You're right on all accounts. I know how much I hurt Allen, and I know how much I hurt myself. To be honest, if he was smart, he'd toss me out and never let me back in." He looked at me with regret then, and sighed. "But, I love Allen. I love him with every fiber of my being."

He turned back toward Mom, who stood frozen while he spoke. "The fact that I do love him is why I ran. I've explained all this to Allen. I've tossed aside everyone who's ever mattered to me at some point in my life. The fear inside me that the people I love will get rid of me, it's all-consuming, and it's also difficult to know that's what

I'm doing when I'm doing it. I can't promise I won't screw up again, and I may well freak out again, but if it helps, my siblings are onto me, Allen and Miss Margaret are too, and it seems so are you. And I've already arranged to talk to a therapist, one who works with my sister, Olivia, and specializes in kids who've grown up in foster care. I know I still have a lot to work through, and this isn't the perfect fairy-tale kind of love story you'd want for your son, but with the past I have, it's all I've got to offer."

I leaned over and kissed his cheek then, my love for him greater than ever. He really was trying, and that's all anyone could ask of him. Mom plopped back on the chair, and said, "I still want to be mad at you, but either you're as amazing as you sound, or you're the best con artist in the world. Gib, honey, I'm sorry about the people you lost when you were little, but I know Margaret. She's told me about her sister, Ruby, and I've met and adore your siblings. At some point, I think you have to let the past go, and embrace the people who love you unconditionally."

She gave me a meaningful look, acknowledging I was one of those people. Gib smiled over at me and winked. "I'm incredibly lucky, and I think the therapist is gonna help. But, yeah, you're right. I'm very blessed to have these people in my life." He put his arm around me then, and let me snuggle into him.

Mom quickly turned and headed into the kitchen, and I could tell she was wiping at her own eyes. Damn, my boyfriend undid the mom of steel. Talk about impressive.

"Lasagna's done. I'll put it on plates and bring it to the table, if that's okay," she called out from the kitchen.

"Thanks, Mom," I said, then leaned over to whisper in my boyfriend's ear. "You're truly amazing, Gibbon Ridley."

He gave me a sad smile, and I knew he was still feeling bad about what Mom had said. I couldn't really fix that, because she'd spoken the truth. I'd been beyond heartbroken when he left. At least now, if he were willing to try like he'd committed to, maybe neither of us would ever hurt like that again.

Thirty-Five

Gib

"Now, I've set up an appointment for you to talk to my therapist friend that I work with," Olivia told me. *Told*, not asked.

My resulting moan earned me a *don't even start* look from her.

"I don't know how well I'll do with a therapist," I said, and to my surprise, she laughed.

"You'll suck at it, probably worse than me or Chase. God knows you suck at emotions more than us."

"Hey," I said, but laughed when she looked at me with her *am I wrong* look.

As it turned out, I liked the therapist instantly. Although, I didn't really have time to drive to her office in Jackson, I was able to do a virtual session with her. She'd let me explain my reaction to Olivia and Chase's marriage, then to how I'd been processing my relationship with Allen. Once I was done explaining it all, she asked me to think about other times I'd pulled away when afraid of being rejected.

Of course, that opened up a discussion about friendships I'd spurned in high school and college. I also had to admit the times I'd resisted letting a guy get to know me beyond a one-night stand. By the end of the first session, it was clear I was keeping everyone at arm's length.

Tears filled my eyes, and I couldn't help breaking down when she asked me to consider the consequences for all the people I'd pushed away, the last year notwithstanding. I was not particularly emotional, and sometimes I thought I lacked some basic emotional skills. I was beyond feeling mortified for sobbing in front of a stranger at the moment, though.

"I hated knowing that Olivia and Chase were hurt when I abandoned them." Tears flowed afresh when I added, "Then, I hurt Allen."

"Gib," she'd said, "Allen has been a breakthrough for you. This is a big deal, Gib. It sometimes takes years for people to grasp the concepts of how their internalized pain is projected onto others."

After that, we scheduled a session for every Monday, since I still had the day of the week off work. She advised me things would get worse before they got better and to call whenever the emotions became too much. I had to use her number more than once as I processed all my confusing and conflicting pent-up emotions, but she helped me put words to them.

I came to realize I was basically still a damaged kid, pretending to be an adult. My therapist told me the only way to avoid repeating old mistakes was to let those I cared about point out when I was freaking out or trying to run away, which I knew they would, because they already had. I was freaking lucky I had people in my life who forgave me, or more importantly, were prepared to give me a second chance.

After the uncomfortable but necessary meal with Allen's mother, I became a frequent supper guest at the house whenever our schedules aligned. As it turned out, Catherine was a fantastic cook, and we usually chatted about how Allen's and my residency programs were going.

One evening, when Catherine told us that her father had decided to sell their family's hotel business, Allen sat up in his chair.

"Mom, really? Are you okay with that?"

She nodded. "Honey, I'm the reason he's selling it. Gib, do you know the story of our company?" she asked.

I didn't, so I shrugged and shook my head.

She smiled and began telling me about her ancestor Patrick Byrne, who'd survived the sinking of his ship as it crossed from Ireland to New York. "He lost his entire family," she said, and I immediately knew she was telling me this story for a reason.

"Patrick's mom, Alice, had been hired to work for the wealthy hotel owner Reginald Fitzgerald. She wrote to him after her husband died in a factory fire, asking if he'd let her and her kids work for him for room and board.

Patrick's story is one of tragedy and luck. Although he lost his mother and siblings in the shipwreck, he survived, and Reginald adopted him, and began showing him the ropes of the business."

The wine we'd been drinking with supper had given all three of us a nice buzz, and I sat back enjoying the story. There was probably a point to it, but at the moment, it just felt nice to hear Catherine sharing so much about her and Allen's family.

"Reginald had arrived in New York and gone to work in a hotel owned by a total jerk of a man. Over the years, he pulled together enough money and influence that when the owner died, he was able to purchase the hotel from the man's widow. Looking back over his history, I think we can assume he was gay. The stories go that women always fancied him, but he rejected them all. At the time, it was said he was too focused on work to want a wife." She chuckled, before adding, "I'm sure there were plenty of men who could tell us stories, though. I wish I could track them down. Our family does have pictures of him, at least, so someday ask me to show you those. He was a tall, lean, and dashingly handsome man."

I smiled as she digressed, then noticing she'd lost the thread of the story, she quickly recovered, by saying, "Regardless, Reginald had no heirs when Patrick, my grandfather, came into his life. Patrick was over forty when he married my grandmother, and my dad was born. I barely remember him from when I was a little girl, but he was standoffish and distant even then."

She looked over at me and I knew she was about to draw the comparison. "I see some similarities with your own story, now I think about it. Reginald died right before Patrick got married and left him, not only the New York hotel, but several others in New Jersey and Massachusetts. Dad and Grandpa grew the business, and when Grandpa Patrick died, my father expanded into Europe. For us, the business represented someone who'd lost it all, then literally scratched and saved to build an empire. It was a forgone conclusion that I'd follow in my dad's footsteps. I didn't want that for Allen. I wanted him to be able to choose his own path. Of course, had I known he was going to follow his father into medicine, I might have been more inclined to give in to the pressure my dad put on me to involve him in the business." She winked at Allen, who just shook his head. "Anyway, now Allen has chosen not to pursue the hospitality business, I told Dad it was time to sell. I want to be free to explore the world without having to work. Although I'm proud of our heritage, running a huge corporation was never my dream."

I was so amazed by her story. There really were interesting parallels between my life and Allen's great-grandfather. I couldn't help but feel empathy for the man who'd lost his family so tragically.

"Is your father upset about you wanting to sell?" I asked, more to distract myself from the melancholy I was beginning to feel.

She nodded. "Of course, he's invested his entire life and mine, for that matter, into it, but he'll be eighty-five this year, and Mom is fed up with the whole thing too. He should've retired years ago. I'm not going to make his mistake, though. I'm going to retire now, and enjoy what life has to offer."

I turned toward Allen to see his reaction, and all I saw was acceptance of his mom's decision. Allen seldom talked about his family's business or his grandfather. Even though his father drove him insane, he talked about the man all the time. I assumed his grandfather rarely came up for discussion, because they weren't very close.

"What will you do after the company sells?" I asked.

She sighed. "Well, I'm not sure. I've thought about a couple things, but at least for a while, I want to find a nice place to curl up and read all the books I've never had time to read, then I'll see what comes after that."

I didn't spend the night at the house. I could tell it would've made Allen nervous, and to be honest, I felt strange sleeping with Allen with his mom under the same roof.

He had to be at work the next morning, so I left early, hoping to give him time to get enough rest. I, however, had the following day off.

Instead of going to Olivia and Chase's, I decided I'd pay Miss Margaret a visit. It was about time I shared some of this new insight I'd had, not that any of it was going to be news to her, she had raised me for a good portion of my life, after all.

Thirty-Six

Allen

AFTER THE COMPANY SOLD, Mom moved into her own place not far from Miss Margaret and her fiancée, Emma. Franklin, unbeknownst to me, was where a lot of famous country music singers also lived. As I drove to see her new house, I almost fell over when I saw the mansion she'd purchased.

"Um, Mom. Why do you need such a big house?" I asked.

"It's an investment," she said. "The man who owned it was going bankrupt and needed to sell it fast."

"Okay, but how much are you going to have in it before it sells?"

"Baby, don't worry about me, I got a huge chunk of the proceeds from the sale of the company. So, trust me, I can afford this."

I knew she could. Mom had never had an issue with money. That was why, when she'd left my dad, she only asked for what was rightfully hers. The financial split was the only amicable thing about their separation.

"Where are Grandma and Grandpa moving now the Manhattan hotel has been sold?" I asked.

"Nowhere, they have a lifetime deed on their apartment. It was a stipulation of the sale. Besides, we purposely sold it to a developer who's turning the whole building into an apartment complex. That old building is no longer considered a high-end hotel like it used to be. It creaks and cracks like the old lady she is."

I wasn't close to Mom's folks. In fact, I hadn't seen them in years. When Mom refused to force me to be involved with the business, Grandpa had thrown a fit and disowned us both. Well, until he realized that by ostracizing Mom, he'd lost the only person who was running the business at the time. When they reconciled, she kept me away from him.

My dad's parents were never close to us either. They enjoyed their retirement and traveled most of the year. We used to spend those dreaded family vacations together, but when my parents divorced, Dad remarried and my brother Lance came along, they decided kids were too distracting, and stopped going with us.

Sometimes I wondered what it would be like to be Fiona, whose grandparents were typical Irish folks who loved her and sent her horrible gifts we made fun of, but that Fiona got giddy about anyway.

I sighed as I thought about the fact that my mother provided the only constant warmth in my life. She drove me insane, but I loved her with my entire being, and never doubted she loved me right back. Other than being temporary roommates, she was now living less than an hour away for the first time since high school, and that was a comforting feeling.

"So," I said to Gib one night, about a month after Mom had moved out, "I think it's time you moved back in."

Gib smiled. "Is that so?"

"Yes," I said as I pushed a package of pulled pork barbeque toward him. I'd driven out to his favorite barbeque place in the boondocks just to buy it as a way to entice him into agreeing to my plan.

Gib ignored the food and leaned over to kiss me. "Is that something you're really ready for? I mean, I'm still a fucked-up mess, you know."

"Yeah, well, we all are, but I miss you too damned much. I want to wake up wrapped in your arms every morning like we used to."

Gib smiled, and whether the barbeque helped or not, I knew I'd managed to talk him into it. I was confident we were on a better path now, especially since he was in therapy, and there was no denying I still craved his touch.

For some reason, even when we fell asleep apart, we ended up in a tangle of arms and legs before the night was done. I couldn't even begin to express how much that kind of tangible connection helped me get through the day, let alone deepened our connection as a couple.

Most of the drama surrounding my residency evaporated when I began working directly for Dr. Jeffers. As strange as it sounded, it took some getting used to not having to constantly watch my back, or wait for the next shoe to drop. Now, I was just like any other resident, including being near the bottom of the ladder as far as seniority went. Dr. Jeffers's involvement hadn't changed that, and to be honest, I was happy. I wanted to pull my weight and had only ever wanted a level playing field to do so.

By the following spring, both Gib and I were more than ready to head to Martha's Vineyard to spend time with Fiona and Alexi. It was Gib's final year of residency, although he was hoping to follow it up with a fellowship.

I was more than a little jealous about that. My pediatric residency would officially end this year, but I still had two more years to go in emergency medicine.

My hospital had the only fellowship program close enough for Gib to feel comfortable applying to, but it was even more exclusive than the regular residency program. They only took four physicians a year into their geriatric fellowship.

Gib had applied, but had yet to hear yes or no.

Our relationship had blossomed over the past year. We enjoyed each other like never before. He'd tease me about how I'd changed while playing doctor, but in truth, the change was all in him. He'd become open and forthcoming. When he freaked out about something, he admitted it before shutting down, and on the few times he did shut down, he went to therapy, then he came home and talked about why.

I was living my dream. I had a job I loved, worked with people I enjoyed, and had the man I wanted more than life itself by my side. I didn't think life could get any better.

GIB

JUST TWO MORE MONTHS of my residency to go and I'd be a full-fledged doctor. Even though I'd been acting as one for more than a year, I still couldn't express how happy I was to have this part of my life completed. Another chapter was about to begin... hopefully in more ways than one.

I had spoken to Fiona and Alexi, and told them I planned to pop the question when we were all together on Martha's Vineyard. They'd both freaked out, of course, but they were all for it. I just prayed Alexi wouldn't let the cat out of the bag, or worse, tell Allen's dad, who might somehow intervene.

I was a nervous wreck as we flew from Nashville to Newark. Fiona and Alexi met us at the airport like they had the first time, but instead of driving to the vacation home, the four of us spent the night at the flat they now shared in Manhattan. Seeing firsthand how happy Fiona and Alexi were as a couple made me all the more thankful Allen and I had reconciled, and we could all get together again, as if no time had passed.

We arrived at the Vineyard by noon the following day, thanks to Alexi forcing us all out of bed at the crack of dawn. I'd come to love the place. It was touristy, of course, but it was also picturesque and relaxing. The ocean was delightful, the warm sun was peaceful, and it always felt so right to be with our friends again.

The next day, we were all lying on blankets chatting about our crazy lives, and the fact that we were almost done with our residencies.

I'd applied for a fellowship in geriatrics, but I hadn't told Allen the latest news yet, because it happened right before we left. Brenda, the nurse practitioner I'd worked with since coming to the clinic, had finished her MBA, and was immediately hired as the health center's CEO after the previous one resigned. One of Brenda's first decisions as the boss was to officially offer me a job as a physician in the clinic. I hadn't said yes, wanting to get the opinions of my three closest friends before making such a big decision, but I was seriously considering it.

When the conversation died down, I leaned up on my elbow, and decided this was the time to bring it up.

"So," I began, looking at Allen. "Before I left, Brenda offered me a job as a full-time physician at the clinic. I didn't have time to tell you, and didn't want to on the plane, but if I take it, I'll be forgoing my fellowship."

I glanced around the group, before continuing, "I'm hoping you'll give me advice on what you think I should do."

Allen smiled. "I knew they were going to ask you. You're too good at what you do, and of course, Brenda adores you."

I chuckled, before saying, "She adores the money I bring in."

"It is a business," Alexi said, all business herself all of a sudden. "What will the fellowship do for you, Gib?"

"It'll better prepare me to serve the older community, of course. It'll also make me more desirable as a specialist."

"It's unlikely you'll make more money," Fiona said. Allen and I looked at each other and smiled. Fiona was always about the bottom line. She'd never understood why I'd gone into family medicine, considering how much less it paid than other specialties.

"No, it's unlikely to make a difference regarding salary."

Allen leaned up and stretched, before asking, "What do you want to do?"

I shrugged. "To be honest, I like where I'm at. I like the work and the responsibilities. I like the patients. The fellowship would be nice, but given a choice between taking this job and spending another year in training, I think I'd rather take the job."

"Then, that's what you should do," Allen said, and as I looked at my friends, they all nodded in agreement. I could've sworn Alexi, at least, would've been pushing for the fellowship, but even she agreed with the others.

I lay back on the blanket and sighed. "Thank God, I'm so tired of school!"

"Preach, sweetheart, preach," Allen said, causing the two women to laugh.

"When did you start calling people 'sweetheart'?" Fiona asked. "You're becoming a Southern hick!"

"Hey, show some respect. You have a bona fide hick here, after all!" I said, pretending to take offense.

Alexi laughed and patted my hand. "Yeah, but you're an adorable hick, so we overlook it."

I rolled over so I could see her, and stuck my tongue out before rolling back and closing my eyes.

"Who's gonna call for pizza? I'm starving!" I said, and our serious conversation changed back to vacation chitchat just like that.

THIRTY-EIGHT

ALLEN

O N FRIDAY NIGHT, EVERYONE except me wanted to go to a fancy freaking restaurant for dinner. "I feel like you all are trying to summon my father," I said indignantly.

The vote being three to one, I lost. We piled into Alexi's car, and took the ferry over to Nantucket and the highly acclaimed restaurant there. I mean, the place was spectacular with its ocean-front views, but who wanted to spend that much time in a car?

Anyway, I checked my attitude enough that I could enjoy one of the last days of our vacation. We had a reservation, and I secretly thanked my friends for having the foresight to at least remember to do that. Otherwise, we'd have driven there for nothing.

In a strange move for him, Gib ordered two bottles of Champagne. When the server brought the wine and poured four glasses, I looked over to Gib, and found my boyfriend kneeling beside my chair. My heart began to beat fast.

When I glanced at Alexi and Fiona, both women had goofy grins on their faces, the kind they always got when we watched one of their hokey romantic comedies.

Gib cleared his throat. "Allen, I'm an idiot when it comes to relationships." Alexi and Fiona, as well as several people seated at tables around us, giggled. "But, in all my life, I've never met a man I love as much as I do you. You not only put up with all my crap, but you seem to love me in spite of it."

Gib reached into his pocket, pulled out a ring box, and asked, "Allen, would you do me the honor of marrying me?"

I was shocked, to say the least. My heart was leaping up and down inside my chest. My mind was screaming *yes, yes, yes*! But, my mouth was stuck on dumb.

When Gib's face fell, it was enough to prompt me out of my stupor. I leaped out of my chair and dropped to the floor before planting a huge kiss on his gorgeous face. The tears were streaming at that point, his and mine, but words were still outside my ability. At that moment, all I could do was nod and cry.

This really was my dream come true. I was going to be Gib Ridley's husband.

After blubbering for several more minutes, Gib pulled me up and sat me back down on the chair. He pulled his over, so it was right next to mine, and the four of us made a toast. Alexi, of course, being the one to offer it.

"Here's to a long and domesticated life!" she said, and we all drank.

When I was finally calm enough to speak, I leaned into Gib, and said, "You shocked me. I'm sorry I wasn't able to respond, but, yes, yes, and more yes! I love you with all my heart, and I can't wait to be your husband."

Gib smiled and leaned in to kiss me, almost as intensely as I'd kissed him earlier.

A few minutes later, the server, a slim, attractive man, came over and handed Fiona her phone. "I think I got it all," he said, and winked at Gib and me before heading to another table.

"You recorded all of that?" I asked, not knowing whether to be upset or pleased.

"You know I did," she said matter of factly. "You'll thank me for it when you see how sweet that entire thing was!"

I chuckled and snuggled into my fiancé. "Oh, shit," I said. "I forgot to put the ring on." I took the ring box off the table, and really looking at the ring for the first time, sucked in a breath. It was beautiful. The Celtic knot swirled artistically around a very discreet sapphire that sparkled in the low light of the restaurant. It was understated, much like my Gib, and therefore it was perfect.

When he noticed me admiring it, Gib said, "I bought it after your mom told the story about your ancestor coming over from Ireland and almost dying. I thought it was appropriate for us, because that tenacity seems to be something you've inherited."

Tears slipped past my defenses again. "You know Mom is gonna be crazy about this, right?"

He cleared his throat and chuckled nervously. "Well, she might've been involved in helping me pick it out."

I stared at the man I'd fallen so incredibly in love with. "You had Mom help you find my engagement ring? And she didn't tell me?"

He nodded. "She knew a perfect jeweler from Dublin. Are you mad at me?" he asked.

I laughed out loud, causing several people in the restaurant, who were clearly still buzzing from the spectacle, to turn toward us. Ignoring them, I said, "Dude, you involved one of the few people I love more than life itself to help pick out my engagement ring, and you think I'd be mad? No, you incredible man, I'm not mad. In fact, thank you *so much* for including her."

Pride vibrated off Gib, and if I hadn't already been insanely in love with him, I would be now for sure.

THIRTY-NINE

GIB

THE PROPOSAL WAS MAGICAL in every way. As Alexi and Fiona had suspected, Allen was pissy about having to go to a fancy restaurant, which just added to the overall fun of what we were doing. It also added to my fears that he'd say no.

Alexi, Fiona, Miss Margaret, Olivia, Chase, and Catherine had all told me repeatedly he would never say no... that he'd confided in all of them how much he loved me. That still didn't alleviate all the doubt I had.

Months ago, as Allen and I sat on the riverbank looking out over what in ancient times was a Native American city and resurrected our relationship, I had decided I was going to propose to him. I initially thought I'd take him back there to propose, but the women in my life all said no, because that was where I'd confessed my sins. Allen probably wouldn't see it as a romantic spot.

Then, I thought I might propose to him in Nashville, but no place felt right. When I mentioned, off the cuff, that I should propose to him while at Martha's Vineyard, both Alexi and Fiona were ecstatic with the idea, and it felt right to me too.

In the end, my proposal played out as it was meant to, on a trip to one of our favorite places and surrounded by our friends. We spent the rest of the night laughing and planning the wedding. I thought we all knew once Olivia, Miss Margaret, and Catherine got the go-ahead, though, they'd be doing most of the planning.

That was fine by me, of course. I knew next to nothing about weddings. As long as I got to marry this incredible man, I'd be beyond happy. I still couldn't believe he'd actually said yes. The amazing, smart, and handsome Allen McCartney was going to be my husband. How could I be that lucky?

"Olivia, it's fine! If you keep trying to get my hair to sit down, you're gonna give me a bald spot," I fussed.

"You've always had unruly hair."

"It's part of my charm," I said sarcastically.

Chase came over and took Olivia by the arm. "Why don't we go and give him a minute."

I chuckled when Olivia looked at Chase like he'd grown horns. "He'll never get ready."

"I've been getting ready for twenty-nine years, Olivia, I'm sure I can get ready now," I said as Chase pulled her out of the room, although I could tell it was taking a lot of self-control for her to allow him to do so.

I sighed and sat heavily on the chair in the small room off the side of the chapel. I really was about to marry my sweetheart. It'd been one year since I'd proposed, and the world had been turned upside down since then.

As we suspected, the women in our lives took over the wedding planning, and it all went fine until they began disagreeing about things. That'd been more than Allen could handle, so he took control, giving everyone duties, but managing the rest himself.

He was as busy as he'd ever been, but the man was nothing if not tenacious. I was, of course, useless when it came to most of the planning. I did my best, but for the most part, it just felt like much ado about one event. No, I'd never say that out loud. This was a massive event in my life, but probably like any stereotypical guy, I'd have been just as happy standing in front of a Justice of the Peace in the local courthouse.

A lonely horn blew over Nantucket Sound, and I realized maybe I was wrong about that. The setting was magical. We'd rented the hotel attached to the restaurant on Nantucket where I'd proposed to him in the first place, and it was filled with Allen's family and mine.

I'd spent hours before everyone arrived sitting out on the wide front porch just enjoying the raw New England beauty steeped in centuries of history. It looked out over the water and watching the ferries coming and going was calming.

My family was all participating in the wedding. Miss Margaret was giving me away. Olivia and Chase were standing up with me. Chrissy was the ring bearer, and the twins the flower girls.

Fiona and Alexi decided to stand with Allen, just so it was even on both sides, and both his mother and father were giving him away. It had been quite a tense few days figuring that one out. His mom was never going to be okay after, and I quote, "I've done all the fucking work raising Allen, while he sat around being a total ass."

I couldn't disagree with her, because he'd been an ass about everything regarding the wedding as well. At first, he refused to acknowledge that we were going to be married. Allen basically told him he could shove it when we hadn't received confirmation back two months after mailing our wedding invitations.

Of course, his dad's wife had intervened and confirmed, saying either they'd be there, or his father would be looking for a new wife. I loved that woman. She was one hundred percent pure sass, and luckily, Mr. McCartney paid attention to what she said.

It wasn't like his father didn't like me. He'd come to visit after we'd first moved in with each other, and he invited me to go on their family vacations, which Allen could never get time off for. I think it was more that he didn't want Allen to *marry* me, which to be honest could've been because I was a man, or a lowly foster kid. With him it was hard to tell what part of me he liked least.

When he finally decided to be involved, he wanted to pay for everything. Both Catherine and Miss Margaret refused wholeheartedly. "He will not come in here throwing his money around, then use it to control everything," Catherine had said. Miss Margaret said she intended to finance my wedding to keep from being haunted by her sister, which she was convinced Mrs. Simmons would do if she "neglected her parental duties."

She'd paid for Olivia and Chase's wedding, and had said something similar then. Of course, knowing Mrs. Simmons, I was guessing she could've been right about that. Our foster mom had been extremely attached to weddings in our community while we were growing up. Often, she'd been the one to play the piano, or set up the music for the ceremonies.

The drama with Allen's family continued to ebb and flow. I would swear weddings and funerals were the two things that could create the most chaos in a family. "Why aren't we eloping?" Allen had asked me when the family tension was at its worst.

"'Cause, you are a princess that deserves her beautiful wedding," I said, teasing him.

Allen stuck his tongue out at me, but then nodded, because it was true.

"Gib, honey, it's time," I heard Miss Margaret say through the door, snapping me back to the present.

"I'm almost ready," I said, which meant I was going to run to the restroom one last time before going down. I had a strange and irrational fear that I'd have to pee halfway through the ceremony, and would either forget my lines or have to excuse myself.

I'd mentioned that to my therapist, and she said it was probably symbolic of my fear of failure, because of things I couldn't control.

Whether or not that was the case, I wasn't taking any chances.

After washing my hands and splashing water on my face, I went back out, took Miss Margaret's arm, and let her lead me into the chapel.

FORTY

ALLEN

I'*M NOT GONNA CRY, I'm not gonna cry!* I kept saying to myself again and again, but the moment I saw Gib walking arm in arm with his foster mother, I lost the battle and had to accept the tears that slowly dripped down my face.

He was utterly handsome in the tux Miss Margaret had purchased for him. The rich blue color of his bowtie brought out the electric blue of his normally hazel eyes.

His face lit up in a smile when he spotted me, and my tummy went all queasy like it used to when I first met him. Somehow, he still had that effect on me all these years later.

Dad and Mom had walked me in earlier, with Fiona and Alexi leading the way. Gib's siblings had come in shortly afterward. The wedding planner Miss Margaret had hired when things had gotten sort of out of hand with Mom and Dad had told us it would make the ceremony feel more meaningful.

I wasn't sure whether she was right or not, but seeing Gib come in had certainly caused the emotions to well up inside me.

Once Gib was next to me, he leaned over and kissed my cheek, before asking, "You ready for this?"

I nodded and winked, then leaned into him as the minister began.

I managed to stem my tears at least to a slow trickle, until Gib took my hand to say his vows, then the tears flowed freely.

"Loving you has been one of the most amazing surprises in my life, Allen. You've been a steadfast force since we met..." He paused for effect before slipping the ring on my finger. "I promise to be faithful to you. I also promise to be loyal and committed. But, the promise I make that is the most heartfelt is that I promise, no matter what happens, to love you unconditionally."

I sighed heavily and the audience chuckled. I really was stupidly lovestruck by this man.

"Gib, you complete me. It's hard for me to express just how much a part of me you've become. Of course, I promise to be loyal and faithful, and to love you forever, but mostly, those are things I've already promised and have given to you. But, on this momentous day, I also promise to be the best companion and husband I can be. I promise to always be your one!"

I was struck once again with a bout of emotions when I looked up to see tears falling from Gib's eyes. I winked at him as I slipped the ring on his finger, then laced my fingers with his.

"Then, without further ado—" the minister said, "—by the power vested in me by the state of Massachusetts, I now pronounce you husbands."

He didn't have to give us permission. Gib had already pulled me into an embrace, and was laying on one of his mind-blowing kisses.

"Anxious to get on with the good stuff," the minister mumbled, and the people in the front row, who were close enough to hear him, giggled.

When we pulled apart, the minister took us by the shoulders, turning us around to the crowd and announced, "Ladies and Gentlemen, I now present to you Allen and Gib McCartney."

Gib McCartney. I'd been saying that name repeatedly to myself over the past year. He had added Ridley as his middle name and taken my surname as his own. He'd been matter-of-fact about it, saying, "I don't know or have a relationship with my Ridley family. I'd have become a Simmons if they'd adopted me, but I love the idea of taking your name, especially since you come from such amazing people."

Of course, I wasn't sure I thought of us as amazing, but whatever the reason, I felt beyond honored.

The reception was a whirlwind of cake, toasts, and happy moments. Everything ended up being a blur for me as I snuggled into the amazing man who'd become my husband. I didn't worry too much though, since Mom had hired what looked like a freaking movie crew to film and document every moment.

When it was finally over, Gib and I slipped into our little rental car, crossed on the ferry, and spent the night in a hotel next to the airport. Dad, of all people, had booked us a flight to Greece for our honeymoon. He'd even hired a yacht to take us around the islands.

Gib had never been there, and I'd been so often I felt like I knew the place by heart.

We didn't do much sightseeing. Mostly, we spent our days lounging on the boat, or swimming in the crystal-blue waters. Dad had booked us a few dinner reservations as well, even though we'd both have rather stayed on the boat and eaten what our gourmet chef prepared. Gib was diplomatic when I complained, though, saying, "It's good to get off the boat from time to time."

Two full weeks later, we flew back to Tennessee to resume our lives. It shouldn't have felt different, seeing as Gib and I had already been living together, but it *was* different. Somehow, being married had brought us even closer. We were more at home, I thought, than we were before.

Another noticeable change was Dad now treated Gib more like family. He began pressuring him to come to family events just as much as he had me. Of course, Gib just laughed it off and never hesitated to give my dad some lip, although always in good humor. Even though my father was as stoic as ever, I could tell he was impressed and liked my husband.

My brother, Lance, well, that was a different story. He'd basically refused to come to the wedding, but as an adult, he could do whatever he pleased. I wouldn't say it didn't hurt my feelings, because it did. He might not like me, but he was still my brother, and seeing Olivia and Chase standing next to Gib caused my heart to break a bit that Lance hadn't felt it necessary to even show up.

As it was, Gib had only met him a couple times, once at my graduation, and once when he'd come home with me for Christmas, but Lance had left early that night. As much as I tried to convince myself not to mourn the brotherly relationship we'd never had anyway, his continuing rejection still stung.

FORTY-ONE

GIB

WORK AT THE CLINIC was absolutely no different now than it had been during my residency. Being a staff physician meant getting paid a real salary for my work, which was a welcome change, but I was still the newest guy there, so I was still on-call more than the other doctors, and I still worked most Saturdays.

I didn't mind. I never had minded, not really. I loved my work, and my patients, for the most part, seemed to like me too.

I did have two guaranteed days off a week now, though, which I hadn't had as a resident. So, I spent Sundays with my husband—it was still hard to believe he and I were married—and Mondays with my siblings. I had every other Saturday afternoon off too, although I remained on-call. I would usually meet Miss Margaret and her wife Emma in Franklin, or they'd meet us all back at the old Victorian to visit Olivia, Chase, and the girls.

I loved having my family close by. Having a husband and a loving family meant everything to me. It was what propelled me through life. A life that was finally going right. Finally, filled with everyone I loved and who loved me back.

I guess that was why when I got a frantic call from Miss Margaret, I thought my world had ended.

Chase had been the public defender for a lowlife drug dealer and Nazi sympathizer who'd moved into the area, then promptly got arrested for attacking and killing a man during a concert when the guy allegedly looked at his girlfriend. The victim had been there with his wife and toddler and two other couples.

All the evidence pointed to Chase's idiot client being trigger-happy, so the court case wasn't going well for him. The guy was out on bail, and Chase had warned him to get his house in order, because he was likely to be found guilty. The man had immediately blamed Chase.

It all happened early Saturday morning during the final week of the trial. Olivia and Chase had left the girls with Miss Margaret and Emma, and had gone back home to enjoy a rare morning alone.

The neighbors reported seeing a nondescript white van pull up to the house before hearing gunfire.

By the time the EMTs arrived, both Olivia and Chase were gone.

I was at work when Miss Margaret called, and I'd almost ignored my ringing phone. I'd had two more patients to see, but I decided if she was calling, it must be important.

"Hidy, Miss Margaret, how can I help..." I halted my silly greeting the moment I heard her crying. "Miss Margaret, is everything okay?"

I heard her sniff, then Emma took the phone from her. "Gib, honey, no... it's not okay. I wish I could make this easier, but Olivia and Chase..."

A loud ringing in my ears nearly drowned out Emma telling me my siblings had been killed.

I hung up the phone, not even sure I'd said goodbye. I couldn't think, the buzzing sound growing louder and louder.

I couldn't get myself to process... my stomach began to roil, and before I knew what was happening, I'd thrown up into the trash can next to the nurses' station.

"Doctor McCartney, are you okay?" Mrs. Phillips, my medical assistant, asked.

"Um..." I said, wiping the vomit from my lips. "Um... no. I'm... um..."

I could feel people gathering around me, and looked up in a daze to see Brenda rushing over. She'd been at the clinic that morning for a staff visit, as she did every so often since taking over as CEO.

"Mrs. Phillips, let Doctor Ferguson know he's going to have to take the rest of Doctor McCartney's patients," she said authoritatively, before leading me to the restroom.

I didn't remember much, other than Brenda giving me a cold, wet towelette, which I held to my head. I kept my head lowered to prevent myself from fainting.

By the time Allen arrived to pick me up, I'd convinced myself I was overreacting. I had just heard it wrong. I needed to call Miss Margaret and find out what had really happened. Maybe I should just call Olivia or Chase, although he never answered his phone. I could call them, though. They'd straighten all this out. I was staring at my phone when Allen knelt beside me. I hadn't realized I was still sitting on the restroom floor.

"Gib, I'm here," he whispered.

I looked at Allen and refused to believe the pain I saw in his eyes. "It's not really happening, right? We're going over to see them this afternoon. They're coming to Miss Margaret's to pick up the kids. Miss Margaret misunderstood. I know that's what's happened."

Allen pulled me to him and wept, although I couldn't. No, it had to be a mistake.

I felt numb as we drove to Miss Margaret's. I just kept saying to myself over and over it was a mistake. In what felt like a feverish hallucination, I looked at Allen once, and said, "It'll be put right when we get there."

The lies I'd been telling myself evaporated the moment I saw Miss Margaret sitting in that same horribly uncomfortable chair that'd once been in Mrs. Simmons's formal living room. She looked old and frail as tears streamed down her face.

Seeing her there crying... it meant this was all real. My knees buckled and I collapsed into the straight back chair in the entryway. My sister and brother, the only family I had besides Miss Margaret, were gone.

I must have wailed, because Allen pulled me into a hug, whispering, asking me to calm down, so I didn't scare the girls, who must've been upstairs with Emma, but I couldn't hear him. I couldn't hear anything. I was beyond lost. It took a long time for me to calm down.

Even then, I could hear the mournful sobs coming out of me. Fortunately, Allen was able to get me into an empty bedroom at the back of the house, before my mourning reached the ears of my nieces.

We lay on the bed, Allen holding me as I sobbed for what felt like hours. I must've fallen asleep, because I woke up to an empty bed.

I heard Catherine's voice, which confused me. Why was my mother-in-law here? Then the weight of it hit me again. Olivia and Chase were gone.

I felt the darkness begin to engulf me again, when I heard Chrissy's voice, smaller than usual and very tentative. I hadn't heard what she asked, but I knew then and there I couldn't afford to go down this hole. As much as I wanted to disappear, get lost and never return, I needed to be here for my nieces.

I got up and used the guest bathroom in the hallway, before going out to face my family and the sadness that was all but palpable even from this far away.

When Chrissy saw me, she rushed into my arms, and I lost it again. As I held her, memories of her early childhood when I'd rejected her parents echoed through my head. I looked up at Miss Margaret, who was looking as if she was holding on by a thread herself. The matching expressions we exchanged said it all.

We'd have to manage our grief at a different time and in a different place. Right now, nothing was more important than the three beautiful little girls who'd just had their entire world ripped out from under them.

FORTY-TWO

ALLEN

Miss Margaret and Gib were lost. They spent copious amounts of time together, once they both saw that between Mom, Emma, and me, we could manage the girls.

The girls were so confused. Even though Chrissy was older, she still didn't comprehend the loss, and seemed to be waiting for her parents to come home at any moment, and the twins were no different.

"I want Mama and Daddy to come home," Ruby said, causing poor Emma to choke back tears.

"I know, baby," she said, taking Ruby and then Margie into her arms. "Your mom and dad went to heaven, though, so they can't come home."

Unfortunately, they didn't understand the significance of what that meant, and the girls just kept asking when their parents would be back. The question grew more painful every time they asked, for them and the adults, because the answer never changed, and never would.

Gib's therapist visited at one point, and spent time with each of the girls before pulling Gib aside to speak to him personally. I wasn't sure what happened during their session, but when he walked out, I saw resignation that hadn't been there before. I thought Gib had been fluctuating between acceptance and disbelief until then.

Autopsies had been performed on Olivia and Chase, and bullet fragments had been found that traced to a gun belonging to one of Chase's clients. The son of a bitch confessed shortly after the cops arrested him.

Shortly after that, we held a joint funeral at the church Gib, Olivia and Chase had grown up attending. They were buried side by side in the cemetery adjoining the church. Despite how they'd been killed, the funeral was open casket, which was good, because I didn't think it was until the girls set eyes on their deceased parents that they realized they were never coming back.

Little Margie screamed when we turned to leave following the service. "Mama!" she wailed. "No, Mama!"

It was devastating to experience, devastating to hear. I knew as long as I lived, the anguish of her plea would never leave me.

I carried her from the gravesite, and sat with her on a wooden bench next to the church, opposite the cemetery, and held her as she cried.

Eventually, Gib came and sat beside me. Margie crawled over into his lap and left her feet in mine.

"Are we gonna live with you now, Uncle Gib?" she asked.

Without hesitating, Gib nodded. "Yeah, baby girl, you're gonna live with me and Uncle Allen now."

Up until that moment, I hadn't thought about where the girls would live. I knew Gib was their godfather, and I'd even signed as a witness when Olivia and Chase updated their wills to make him guardian of his three nieces if anything ever happened, but even then, I didn't think, not really, about what that could mean for him *and* me.

I began to freak out, and quickly quashed the feelings. This wasn't the time for that. I couldn't break down when a little girl had just buried her mom and dad. Not just one little girl, but three. Three children. Three girls who would be coming to live with us. *Forever*.

Gib looked up at me, and when I saw concern, I forced myself to smile. He saw right through me, though, and the sadness that'd been so prevalent for the past two weeks was back full-force. I was sure he knew I was freaking out, and instead of making him angry, he was sad.

At that moment, I knew if I forced Gib to choose, he'd have to choose them, and rightly so. Olivia and Chase had entrusted their children to him, and he wouldn't, *couldn't*, let them down. I just had to make sure I didn't force him to choose, because as painful as it'd been for him to put those two incredible people in the ground, that was how devastated I'd be to lose him.

Following the service, the church put on one of the most intense potlucks I'd ever seen in my life. I sat between Mom and Emma, with Margie still clinging onto me for dear life. Ruby sat quietly between Emma and Miss Margaret, and Chrissy sat next to Gib. The two of them had the exact same expression of deep, soul-level grief. Chrissy rarely left Gib's side, and the therapist even said the two of them were on some sort of strange wavelength, and were healing through each other.

People came and offered condolences again and again, then it was over. We piled into a van Mom had rented that could transport us all, and we drove to the old Victorian where the girls had lived with their parents. The home where Olivia and Chase had been murdered.

FORTY-THREE

GIB

I FELT AS DEAD inside as my sister and brother were for real. Despite that, I had to keep things together for Chrissy, Ruby, and Margie. Of course, keeping myself numb was the only way I knew to do that. If I let myself feel, I'd just curl into a ball and let myself die too.

Chrissy clung to me like she had when she'd been a little thing confronted by two screaming siblings. There was something healing about that. Jan, my therapist, told me I should let the girls mourn in whatever way they needed to. That included letting Chrissy be clingy, letting Margie express her emotions as they came, and letting Ruby sit quietly. Each was a legitimate and healthy way to process their loss.

Also on Jan's advice, following the funeral, we all found ourselves back at the house where Olivia and Chase had been killed. The house that had once been filled with memories of our shared childhoods would now be forever linked to the violent deaths of my beloved siblings.

Jan had told me it was healthy to be here where it'd happened, so the entire family could process it. She'd said the girls needed their home for as long as we were able to give it to them.

I called Brenda and told her I wouldn't be able to return to the clinic anytime soon, explaining that with the loss of my siblings, I needed to stay close to the girls for now. Of course, she'd been more than understanding.

Allen had to return to work, or lose his residency. They'd been extremely understanding as well, and gave him two full weeks off. Those were two weeks we'd really needed. He didn't complain when I told him I'd have to stay at the old Victorian with the girls. Instead, he worked out his schedule so he could be there as often as possible too.

We operated like that for two weeks, until Miss Margaret and Emma intervened. "You can't keep that up," Miss Margaret told me. "You're a married man and need to spend time with your husband."

"The girls are my priority," I said. It came out more hateful than I meant.

"The girls are all of our priority, including his," Emma replied, none too gently.

I sighed. I was being overly protective. Somehow in my very messed-up mind, it was almost like I could bring back Chase and Olivia if I took care of the girls well enough. I knew it wasn't healthy, but I still hadn't spoken to Jan about it. I was slipping back into my old ways. Push everything and everyone away. Live in the moment. Don't feel too much.

"We're going to keep the girls during the week, at least until you and Allen can work things out. Besides, it's just over a month until they'll be out of school for the holidays. If you're going to move them, that's the time to do it."

I'd already thought of that since moving them into our house also meant switching schools. However, doing so over the holiday break would hopefully make for a smoother transition than pulling them out in the middle of the semester.

"What if Allen doesn't want to be a dad?" I blurted, which was really at the heart of why I'd pulled back the way I had.

"Have you not spoken to him about it?" Miss Margaret asked.

I shook my head. "It's been crazy here," I admitted.

Both women sighed at the same time. "That's all the more reason for us to take on some of the care for the girls, and give you two a chance to process," Miss Margaret said, in the tone she used when there was to be no argument.

That night, we worked out a schedule, and it did make more sense. I could go back to work at least part-time while Miss Margaret and Emma stayed with the girls during the week.

If Allen and I were going to bring the girls home to live with us, we'd need to have them staying with us some of the time too, but that required a conversation—an awfully long and meaningful conversation.

I left Miss Margaret and Emma in the girls' playroom to wait for them to get home from school, and wandered up to Chase's home office to have my therapy session with Jan.

We talked about how I'd been acting with the girls. I admitted I was being overprotective, and acknowledged I was alienating everyone as a result. Of course, coming to terms with that was the biggest part to work through, but admitting it to Jan helped too.

"So, same time next week?" I asked, and she confirmed before hanging up.

I left the house after the girls got home, telling them I needed to spend some time with Uncle Allen before he started feeling too lonely. To my surprise all three girls nodded. "When will you be back?" Chrissy asked.

I looked over at Miss Margaret, before saying, "I'm going to pick you up to spend the night with us over the weekend, or if Uncle Allen is too busy with work, I'm going to come stay here with you."

They seemed to take it okay, at least, until I pulled out of the driveway. Chrissy called me immediately, crying. "What's wrong, sweetheart?" I asked her.

"You're not gonna come back! You're going to die too." The sound of her uncontrollable sobs filled the car.

"Oh, honey," I said, and turned the car around.

I could see all three of my nieces peeking through the front window as I pulled back up to the house. Chrissy came barreling out the front door as I reached the porch, wrapping her arms around my legs in a fierce hug. We held onto each other until her sobs subsided, then I spoke to all three girls.

"I don't know why we lost your mama and daddy, but I'm here, okay? I'm not leaving," I said, embracing them all in a group hug. "I need to go see your Uncle Allen right now, but I'll be coming back. You have Miss Margaret and Emma here now, and we all love you to bits."

Driving away from them the second time was even harder than the first. I was sure I'd never leave them again if I didn't think my relationship with my husband was worth at least giving the man some time to process this all with me. I had no idea what I was going to do if he said no to taking on the girls. I took a deep breath to dislodge the huge boulder that sat on top of my heart at that thought. *No use fretting over an issue before I know if there even is one*, as Chase had said to me time and time again.

I wiped at the tear that slipped out at the memory, and drove home to have a conversation with my husband about becoming parents to our three little nieces.

FORTY-FOUR

ALLEN

I COULD TELL GIB needed to talk, but he was avoiding it. It wasn't like I didn't know what he wanted to talk about, the girls were now his responsibility, a responsibility he'd signed up for before the twins were even born, and he and I had become a couple.

Regardless, I wanted... no, *needed* him to bring it up. I needed him to ask me, although I was already fully prepared to say yes, but for some reason, it needed to be something he discussed with me, not just assumed.

After Gib found every excuse to not bring it up, I finally said, "Just spit it out, Gib. Stop avoiding what you want to ask."

"I'm such a chicken shit," he said, causing me to chuckle.

"Baby, I love you with all my heart, but you really are!"

He took a long, deep breath. "I know you didn't sign up for this, but I have to decide what I'm going to do about the girls."

I nodded and almost forced him to ask me directly, then decided against it.

"Gib, I knew what I was signing up for when we got married. You told us all while we were in medical school that you were the girls' godparent. If you're asking me if I'm willing to step up as their parent, the answer is yes, of course I am."

Gib's face crumpled at my words, and he broke down. He sat on the edge of the sofa, and wept while I held him. "It's okay, baby, it's okay."

He shook his head. "No, Allen, it'll never be okay. I'm not their parent. They need Olivia and Chase, but I can't be them. It should've been me."

I felt a hot tear slip down my face at the thought. I pulled back and met his eyes, as I said, "No, my sweet husband, it shouldn't have been anyone, but bad people are out there who don't think about what they are doing, not until it's too late. But, sweetheart, those girls *will* be okay. I know they will, because you and I, Mom, Miss Margaret and Emma, we're all gonna make sure they're okay. We can't heal their broken hearts, but we can all help ensure they survive this."

Gib nestled into me like he often did these days. It was almost as if he were trying to pull hope from my soul into his.

"So, you're okay with the girls becoming ours then?"

"Of course, I am, but we're going to have to talk about how we're gonna manage it. I've still got a year left in my residency, and you're working at the clinic."

"I think I need to spend some time not working," he said, with a look of uncertainty. "The girls need structure and consistency. For now, Miss Margaret and Emma are going to live in the house during the week, then we can either go there or bring them here on the weekends, but after the New Year, I think we should bring them here to live with us full-time."

I nodded. I'd already thought we should bring them here, and his plan made the most sense. The girls needed to finish school, and starting here after winter break was a much better way to transition.

"Okay, that sounds like a good plan to me, but, no, I don't think you should quit altogether. We need to meet with my mom, Miss Margaret, and Emma first, to see what they're willing to commit to."

"I just don't see how I'm going to work..."

"Even if you only do one day a week, you need to keep up the practice, because eventually, you'll want to go back," I said, hoping he'd see reason. He'd worked too hard and loved his work too much to give up medicine entirely. Besides, now was not the time to make any more life-altering decisions than were absolutely necessary.

When I saw hope in his eyes, it comforted me. He was willing to sacrifice everything for the girls, but if we all did our part, maybe he wouldn't have to.

We all met on Saturday. I'd taken the day off from the hospital. The girls were spending the night with Miss Margaret and Emma, so when we arrived at the old Victorian, everyone was there, including my mother.

We included the girls in the family meeting, because Gib said our planning was as much about them as it was about us. I knew the twins would lose interest quickly and disappear, but Chrissy was the opinionated one. If she didn't agree to our plans, it could be difficult to work around.

"So," Miss Margaret began. "I officially call our first extended family meeting to order. We are meeting to discuss the future of our family, so who would like to start?"

Chrissy raised her hand, and Miss Margaret nodded to her. "We don't want to leave our home," she said, and the twins sat uncharacteristically still, waiting for us to respond.

Gib cleared his throat, and said, "We're going to work hard to let you stay in your house for as long as we can, but when you were all babies, your mom and dad made me promise that if anything happened to them, I would take you to live with me." He watched the girls, who remained motionless, as he continued, "I talked to Uncle Allen, and he and I both agree that we want you to live with us, just like I promised your parents, but Uncle

Allen works in Nashville, and since he and I are husbands, we need to live together. Do you understand?"

Chrissy nodded, but the sadness was clearly evident in her features. Maybe more than the twins.

Miss Margaret chimed in then. "Emma and I live in Franklin, and Catherine lives just down the road from us, so when you're not in school, we want you to spend time with us too, but like your Uncle Gib said, Franklin isn't close to this home."

Chrissy wiped at her silent tears, and asked, "When do we have to move?"

"We were thinking after Christmas," I said, trying to let the girls know we were all united.

"Can we all spend Christmas together here before we move?" she asked. The hope on her innocent face caused my heart to break.

All the adults in the house nodded. "It seems like that's a yes from everyone, sweetheart," Gib said, and opened his arms so she could snuggle into him for a moment.

The twins came over and hugged both Gib and me before crawling up on the sofa with Miss Margaret and Emma.

"So, it sounds to me like the rest of this family meeting needs to be used to plan for Christmas, starting with your Christmas lists!" I said, immediately shifting the heavy mood in the room.

I went to the kitchen to grab the hot chocolate Emma had made before the meeting started. I found a tray and carried them all into the living room. The girls were in an animated conversation about all the things they wanted for Christmas. Chrissy was writing her own list, while the little ones were dictating theirs to Mom.

The sadness never went away. It was there and would be for a very long time. Having to move them out of the home they'd always known was horrible, and I wished beyond words that the house was closer to work, so they could stay there. I knew Gib was feeling sad about it, and I assumed Miss Margaret was too. Both of them had grown up in this house as well.

When the girls had gone off to play video games, which Emma had set up in the family room, the rest of us sat down and discussed the transition details, and who would keep the girls when.

Everyone agreed that Gib shouldn't quit his job. Franklin was less than thirty minutes from us, so Mom and Miss Margaret both said they could pick the girls up whenever needed. They also offered to spend time with the kids when they weren't at school, giving Gib and me time to continue being newlyweds.

"I really appreciate that," I said, mostly to myself, but everyone heard me and chuckled.

When we left that evening, we had a working plan. For now, Gib was to return to work. The girls would stay with Miss Margaret and Emma at the old Victorian during the week, and they'd spend weekends with us.

Forty-Five

Gib

I WENT BACK TO work, but since I'd been gone for over a month, a new nurse practitioner had been hired and I wasn't needed that much. So, I worked three days a week, and spent the rest of the time between the girls and Allen.

Most Sundays we spent with the girls at our house, preparing them for their lives with us. Luckily, each girl had their own bedroom, since the house had three bedrooms on the upper level, and a big open space Allen and I could turn into our bedroom in the basement for added privacy.

The mid-century house didn't have a huge master bedroom, but it did have its own bathroom, so that became Chrissy's room. The other two rooms were exactly the same size, and were next door to one another. It couldn't have been more perfect for our little family if we'd gone out to shop for it.

Each weekend they spent with us, we did something extra to fix up their rooms, and by Christmas, all their stuff had been moved out of their family home and into ours.

Christmas was spent in the old Victorian, and it was as emotional for Miss Margaret and me as it was for the girls. The home was steeped in memories. The historical society had questioned Miss Margaret about it right after Thanksgiving, and had offered to purchase it from us.

The old house had been the first home in the area that wasn't a log cabin. The first mayor, who'd also founded the town, had built it. He was Miss Margaret's distant ancestor. I knew she struggled with the sale, but none of us lived there any longer, and the girls were just too young to inherit. Selling it to become a county museum was the best possible outcome.

I was pleased when the historical society agreed to purchase the old barn hill property as well. Olivia and Chase had never sold it after moving into the old Victorian, and it had originally been part of the same property. I relished the idea that the historical society might one day build a replica of the old barn and bring the entire property back to its full glory.

Most of the antiques had gone with Miss Margaret when she'd moved out, since Olivia and Chase hadn't been interested in them, and I think Miss Margaret was sure the kids would destroy them. I was more than a little surprised when she told us she'd donated all the original furniture for the future museum, so it would remain authentic.

The historical society had also asked for family photos, including those of Olivia, Chase, the girls, and me. I'd long felt that the old home was a part of all of us, so it was fitting that we be included as part of its history.

Decorating the Christmas tree was exceptionally emotional for all of us, but especially for the girls and me. I wiped at the tears as I hung up the hideous homemade decorations Olivia, Chase, and I had made for each other and Mrs. Simmons when we'd been really little.

The girls were somber too as they hung up the stockings Olivia had knitted for them just the year before.

Christmases were full of memories, and I knew deep down that eventually those memories would be good ones again, but this year, they just reminded us of everything we'd lost.

After Christmas, we spent the following week packing up anything in the house that we wanted to take with us. Most of what we kept were things that'd belonged to Chase or Olivia—things that one day, we all knew the girls would want.

Once we were out, Miss Margaret hired a cleaning company to clean the place until it was spotless, then we moved all the antiques back in that'd sat in the house my entire childhood. While we were setting it all back up, I had more than one emotional breakdown as memories came flooding back of my siblings, Mr. and Mrs. Simmons, and Miss Margaret... our family.

The most intense and ridiculous moment was when Miss Margaret's horrible settee was put back in its place of pride. She looked at me funny when my tears streamed. "What's gotten into you?" she asked.

On a wet chuckle, I admitted how much the three of us had hated it. "Of course, you always made us sit here when we'd been naughty too."

She smiled. "To be honest, I hated that thing too. I almost left it here for the girls to destroy, but too many years of my father fussing at us to keep it clean were hard to let go."

Miss Margaret and I had several moments like that as we put the old home back into its original condition. There was something magical about seeing the place like it'd been when we were little.

I even went to a joke store we used to frequent when we were little, bought a plastic garter snake, and with tears in my eyes, placed it on the bed Mrs. Simmons slept in when we were growing up. When Miss Margaret questioned me, I shook my head, and took several long moments to pull myself together.

When I finally explained to Miss Margaret that the day we found out she was coming to live with us, Olivia had snuck a snake into Mrs. Simmons's bedroom. Miss Margaret surprised me with a full-out laugh. "You young'uns were such a handful."

She wiped at a tear, and sighed. "I miss seeing you three playing together. They are some of my fondest memories."

I was shocked, of course. Most of our lives with her had been about her controlling us, but even so, those were my best memories too. "Now, we just have to make sure the three girls have the same chance to make those kinds of memories."

Miss Margaret nodded, and walked out of the old bedroom and down to the formal living room that was once again full of horribly uncomfortable furniture.

The ringing of the doorbell sent sadness through me, as I knew it was the ladies from the historical society coming to collect our keys. Miss Margaret led them into the newly recreated parlor where I was waiting.

I removed the key from my keyring, and Miss Margaret and I handed over our keys. Miss Margaret quickly told them about the rubber snake, and both women laughed. They'd known us well as children too. Miss Nina had been our fourth-grade teacher, and Mrs. Hart had been our Sunday School teacher. "We promise to leave the snake right where it is. It'll be a great story to share with the kids who come to visit."

Miss Margaret and I held hands as we walked out of the house together for the last time. We were both sad at the closing of a chapter and happy that our childhoods, the good and the bad, would be preserved for posterity.

Forty-Six

Allen

By April, our family was operating as one would expect with three young girls still finding their footing in a new school after losing their parents.

"Girls, come on!" I yelled up the stairs for the third time. Gib was working late at the clinic, and when Mom had volunteered to take the kids, he and I had decided to meet downtown and have a real date that didn't involve nuggets or a Happy Meal. The girls had yet to spend the night with Mom, and she was bound and determined to change that.

"Do you really wanna make Grandma Catherine miss her reservation?" I asked, but got no answer.

It wasn't like the girls were afraid of my mother. She'd demanded they call her Grandma at Gib's and my wedding, which was the first time they'd met her, and she'd made it a point to send gifts to them long before the dreadful loss that made her their foster grandmother.

When I didn't hear any response, I went up and found Chrissy and Ruby working feverishly to remove a curling iron from Margie's hair. The second I walked in, I could smell burnt hair and I moaned inwardly.

I was relieved that one of them had been smart enough to unplug the curling iron. Without saying anything, I quickly disentangled the thing from Margie's hair and began trying to comb it out. It really was no use, though. The singed hair was damaged beyond repair.

"You all should've called me to come help."

The three looked shyly down at the ground, not saying a word. "What is it?" I asked.

"We didn't want to disturb you," Chrissy said.

"Disturb me. Isn't that what you're supposed to be doing right now?" I asked, and teasingly prodded all three of them until I got tentative smiles in return.

"It'll be okay, Margie. I'll call Grandma Catherine and ask her to help figure out what to do about your hair. I'm sure she'll have some magic that'll fix it, but all three of you need to know I'm here for you. I don't know much about hair, but I do know a thing or two about undoing curling irons."

When they looked at me with a confused expression, I told them about when I'd wanted to look like Justin Timberlake. I was trying to curl my hair, not knowing I'd need a perm to achieve anything resembling his signature curls, and then, when their faces still registered mild confusion, I had to explain that Justin Timberlake was a famous singer with equally notable hair.

"My hair was much worse than yours, Margie," I said, chuckling. "Grandma Catherine just shaved it off."

Margie's eyes grew large, and I laughed. "No, she won't shave all your hair off. My hair was too short for a curling iron, so I ended up burning a lot of it. Yours isn't that bad."

That seemed to mollify her, although all three girls were still being strangely quiet. If I was honest, they had been since they'd moved in four months earlier.

I took a picture of Margie's hair and texted it to Mom, then dialed her number before putting the phone on speaker.

"Are you almost here?" Mom asked, instead of saying hello.

"Um, no, we've had a mishap. Can you look at your messages, and tell us what we need to do to fix Margie's hair?"

Margie had begun to cry, probably because I was calling Mom about it, and I quickly went over and put my arm around her shoulder.

"Oh, yes, I see," Mom said. "What happened?" I prodded Chrissy into telling her the whole story. I could tell Mom was trying not to laugh, and when an errant chuckle slipped out, I said, "I know you're thinking about me, and I've already told them what I did."

She laughed out loud. "It was so horrible. Anyway, Margie, baby, don't you worry. We'll put it up in a bun and then tomorrow, I'll take you to my stylist to have it fixed."

"Can she see them on Sunday?" I asked.

"Of course, I'll text her now and tell her I need her."

I'd already packed the girls' stuff for their overnight visit, and it was in the trunk of the car, a car that was clearly way too small for a family. I'd decided Gib and I needed to sell it, and God forbid, purchase a minivan, but we'd been too busy to find the time. I had no idea the lives of elementary-school kids were so busy.

As I piled the girls into the car, still concerned they were being too quiet, I quickly assessed whether I had everything or not before locking the house, and climbing into the driver's seat.

"You girls okay?" I asked. They all nodded. I internally made a note that I needed to have another chat with the therapist. It was like the girls didn't trust me or feel comfortable around me. Before Olivia and Chase died, they were so outgoing and rambunctious all the time, regardless of who they were around.

"Hey," I hedged as we got on the road. "Why are y'all so quiet lately?" I'd asked that before, of course, but I only ever got a shrug. I sighed. "Well, whatever, you were so loud before, I thought you were gonna break my eardrums anyway."

When they didn't giggle, I was concerned. It seemed like they were getting worse.

After we arrived at Mom's house and she'd shown the girls to their room, I pulled her aside to say the girls had been getting more withdrawn around me by the day. "If you can get them to talk to you about it, it'd be helpful," I said.

Mom nodded, but couldn't say much since the girls were coming out of their room.

"Okay, Margie, let's see the damage," Mom said and as she surveyed the hair, she tutted. "Well, let's use one of my ballerina caps and tie this up into a ball. It'll be cute and no one will be any the wiser." She said it with such complete confidence that the girls smiled.

As I left the house, I was struck by how the girls seemed more at ease the moment we got to Mom's place. We really did have to figure this out sooner rather than later.

Forty-Seven

Gib

I T SEEMED LIKE THE entire world had changed since the girls had moved in. The clinic needed me less and less, and to be honest, I was beginning to feel guilty about staying on the payroll.

"I just don't know where you fit, Gib," Brenda admitted.

"Yeah, me neither. I'll tell you what, Allen and I discussed this, and I'm happy to work as a volunteer doctor. That way, you can send me to whichever clinic you feel needs me. I can get away for a day here and there."

She looked sad, but nodded. "I'm afraid that's about the best we can do. Usually, we're begging for doctors, but since we're going to have another resident at the East Clinic, that pretty much puts me above capacity."

"Brenda, it's perfect. I need to spend more time with the girls anyway."

I hoped it would be fine. I was being delicately let go. It wasn't really a negotiation, except that Brenda was a friend, and she was clearly trying not to hurt my feelings.

Now, I had to break the news to Allen, and on the first night in months when we'd actually have time to ourselves.

I pulled up at the restaurant, and was walking toward the front when Allen came up behind me, and slipped his arm into mine. "Perfect timing," he said.

I turned to see him and felt the same thrill I'd had since first meeting him all those years ago. "I love you," I said as I kissed his cheek.

"I love you too, and we have a night alone! Who knew this'd ever happen again?"

As soon as we walked in, we were escorted to a booth, and the server brought out the wine we'd pre-ordered when making the reservation. We clinked glasses and toasted the two of us.

I looked down at my glass, wondering if I should just delay my news until after supper.

"So, what's going on? You have that look again."

"What look?" I asked, and couldn't help cracking a smile.

"The look you get when you have to tell me something and don't want to."

"Am I that easy to read?" I asked, knowing I was pouting. He knew me too well.

"Totally," he said, and smiled. "So, out with it. What do you have to tell me?"

"I've been let go from the clinic. Well, sort of. They don't really need me any longer."

Allen nodded and then sighed like he wasn't surprised. "So, what are you going to do?"

"I'm going to volunteer for now. When the girls are more settled, I'm going to have to find another job."

"Well, it shouldn't be hard. I know primary care is desperate everywhere. You could probably get hired on at the hospital."

I shook my head. "No, I'd prefer not to if I can avoid it. I want to stay in a rural setting, preferably in a town that we live in, so I can get to the girls easily if I'm needed."

"So, you're wanting to move?" he asked.

"Allen, honey, I don't know what I want. I just talked to Brenda today. Besides, after you're done with your residency, you may not be here either."

Allen cringed and shook his head. "No, they offered me a full-time position starting this summer. Doctor Jeffers is looking to retire in a year or two, and he wants to groom me as an attending physician."

I stared at my normally oversharing husband, and asked, "So, how long ago did you get the offer?"

Allen shrugged. "Doctor Jeffers has been talking about it off and on for a year. I just wasn't sure how I felt about it. I mean, on the one hand it would be wonderful, but I'd be required to teach courses or do research. That'd mean more training, which I'm not interested in. Not only that, but I didn't graduate here. It was pretty tough being an outsider when I first started. I'd prefer not to repeat that."

He gave me a pained look, before he said, "I was mostly pretending like it was a joke, not giving it much credibility, but last Friday, Doctor Jeffers asked me to give him a definitive answer soon."

"So, what will it entail?" I asked, confused by how uncharacteristically indecisive my husband was being.

"Much less than what I'm doing now. I'd become a fully credentialed physician, and Doctor Jeffers would start giving me other duties as and when I feel comfortable. Then, when he finally retires, if the hospital likes what I've done, they'd probably offer me the job. But, there's no guarantee. Of course, if they don't offer it to me, I'll be trained and can take on the same job in any number of hospitals around the country."

"That's sort of great, Allen. Why are you resisting it so much?"

Allen thought for a moment, before he said, "I wanted to be more available to spend time with you and the girls. If I take this on, it'll be long hours."

I scoffed. "And that's different how? I mean, we did decide to become physicians, Allen. We knew what the hours were like."

"Yeah, but there's a difference between a normal work week and having to be in charge."

"But, you always said you *wanted* to be in charge."

He looked at me for a long time, as if trying to make up his mind, before saying, "I do, but I want a simple life too."

I reached over and took his hand. "Listen, Allen, there have been huge changes this past year, and those changes have rocked us both to our cores, but don't give up on your dreams. I can see you rising up through the ranks of the hospital or the school if you prefer that, and I guess I always figured you would. It's literally part of your DNA."

Allen moaned. "Don't say that."

"What, that you're following in your dad's footsteps? I'd never say such a thing." I tried sounding sincere, but couldn't help my smirk.

Allen stuck his tongue out at me before lacing our fingers together. "Thanks for being understanding."

"Of course, now let's order. I'm starving."

FORTY-EIGHT

ALLEN

I 'D BEEN STRESSING OVER the whole promotion thing for months, not wanting to even acknowledge it might be real, but a quick conversation with my man about it had me feeling confident again.

Not for the first time, I realized how lucky I was to have Gib as my husband.

We had just finished eating and were about to leave when I got a call from Mom, and answered in case there was an emergency.

"Hey, Mom, what's going on?" I asked.

"Hi, son. Is Gib with you?" she asked.

"Yeah, we're here together. Mom, what's up? Are the girls okay?"

"Yes, they're fine, I just put them in bed, but I need to talk to you and Gib about what they told me."

That made me nervous, but we quickly walked out of the restaurant and got into my car, where I put the phone on speaker.

"Okay, Mom, go ahead. What'd the girls say?"

Mom took a long deep breath and let it out slowly. "So, I know why they've been so distant with you, Allen, and maybe even you, Gib."

We both waited expectantly, trading worried looks before glancing back at the phone.

"You have a teacher problem," she said. I could tell by her voice that my mom was barely controlling her temper.

"Chrissy's teacher has been getting pretty religious, even quoting the Bible each morning, at least that's what she told me when I prodded. But, before that, she said her teacher had told her that you aren't her real uncle and that the state would come and take the girls away from you, especially if she misbehaved."

Gib's face was glowing red, and I could feel his rage, because it burned hot in me too.

"What else did she say?" Gib asked, his tone soft and totally betraying the emotions I saw on his face.

"Well, she told her you were going to hell, and quoted Leviticus. Of course, Chrissy didn't know what Leviticus was and mispronounced it, but it was clear that's what she meant."

"Dear God," Gib said.

"Mom, thanks for telling us. We'll talk to the girls about it tomorrow when we pick them up."

"Well, actually, I was thinking I might keep them overnight tomorrow too. If you're going to confront the school on Monday, it might be good for the girls not to be there when you do, and if *you* don't, *I* sure as hell am."

Gib nodded, and I said, "Yeah, okay, we'll come have breakfast with you in the morning, and bring the girls some extra clothes. Did they say they wanted to spend another night with you?"

She chuckled. "Of course, I bribed them with candy and a movie night. My friend Killen is bringing her daughters over too, so it'll be like a slumber party."

"You're incredible, Mom," I said sarcastically, and she laughed.

"Regardless, you need to handle that teacher before I go slap the woman silly with her own Bible. You know I don't look good in orange, Allen."

I laughed. "Agreed, and if Gib's face right now is any indication, it's gonna get really hot Monday morning."

Forty-Nine

Gib

MY ENTIRE BODY WAS shaking by the time we got home after hearing what Catherine had told us. I knew what Chrissy was saying about her teacher was true, because she wouldn't have known to quote Leviticus. Olivia had been a dictator with the girls' old school, and even the church they attended regarding how they were to act when the girls were around. She'd even taken the girls out of church for a few months when something derogatory about gay people was said during service. Miss Margaret had ended up pulling the stipend her father had donated to the church as well. It was a substantial amount of money, and the pastor had quickly agreed not to preach that sort of sermon again.

The little church was mostly full of open-minded and loving people anyway, so it wasn't like he was preaching to a congregation that actually hated anyone.

Now, less than four months under my care, I'd let the ball drop. The girls were hearing the same hatred, and hearing it on my freaking watch. I'd have that bigoted teacher's hide before this was done.

Allen and I got up the following morning and drove to Catherine's house. She told us, in front of the girls, that they were afraid they'd be taken away, and Allen explained to them that the law wouldn't allow that, and Chrissy's teacher was breaking the law by what she'd said in a public school.

It was amazing to watch as the girls each took a collective breath of relief after Allen told them that.

"Will they put Mrs. Kent in jail?" Chrissy asked.

"No, but she might lose her job," I said, deciding not to mince words. I wanted the girls to know the truth, and although they knew to respect adults, they should also know they had rights, and when a teacher was breaking the freaking law to harass them, they damned-well *needed* to understand those rights.

"I'm going to go speak to your teacher and principal, and find out why she broke the law. It might help if you could tell me exactly what she's been saying, though."

Chrissy nodded and told me everything Catherine had relayed to us last night. The only thing Chrissy hadn't disclosed before was that her teacher had made her stay in from recess a couple times to write lines about how God wanted her to be a good Christian, even if she was being exposed to the devil.

I had to take several breaths before I spoke, so I didn't end up cussing up a blue streak right there in front of the kids. After we'd finished talking, and the girls were in Catherine's theater room watching a Disney movie, I decided to take a long walk alone to cool off.

When I got back, Catherine's friend and two daughters had arrived, and there was a great deal of noise coming from the theater room.

"You okay?" Catherine asked when she saw me.

I shook my head. "No, but by this time tomorrow, I promise I will be."

She smiled a wicked smile. "Wish I could go with you. Want me to go with you?" she asked.

I chuckled. "Not this time, but if things don't go to plan, maybe next time."

Allen and I decided to go to the school as a united front. He was working a late shift, so he didn't have to be at the hospital until eleven in the morning.

We arrived while students were still getting off the bus, and sat in Principal Johnson's office until he'd finished with the morning duties. He was clearly surprised to see us, and asked if we could wait while he made the daily announcements.

I nodded curtly, but didn't respond.

He returned a few minutes later.

"How can I help you two gentlemen?" he asked.

I had taken the time to write down exactly what Chrissy had told me and instead of talking, I pushed a printed copy of my documentation toward him. Allen and I waited as he read it.

As he did so, his face reddened noticeably. When he looked up at us, he said, "This is highly irregular."

"I should hope so, Principal Johnson," I said. "What I need to know now is exactly what's going to be done with this teacher. As you know, we both have very busy schedules, and even less patience for this kind of illegal nonsense. If we need to have an attorney involved, that can be arranged."

"Please wait here," he said, and left us sitting alone in the office. I could hear him speaking to the secretary and asking her to relieve Mrs. Kent, so she could join the meeting.

I'd met the woman at the start of the semester, and she'd seemed nice enough then. She certainly didn't seem to have any issue with us, and when we'd enrolled the girls in the school, Allen and I had done so together.

I knew she was guilty as fucking sin when she walked in, though, because she wore a mixed expression of both fear and arrogance.

When she sat down, the principal grabbed the sheet of paper I'd documented Chrissy's story on and read it out loud.

The woman didn't budge. Instead, she sat stiff-backed in the chair.

"Mrs. Kent, is this true?" he asked.

"I have a Constitutional right to express my opinion," she said to him, now ignoring us completely.

"I have a feeling a court of law may disagree with you," I heard myself respond.

She looked at me coldly then, and said, "I just told the girl the truth."

"You did no such thing. You told her the lies you've convinced yourself to believe. You lied to *my* niece, whom I have legal guardianship over, that I am not her uncle. You lied to *my* niece that if she misbehaves, the state will take her from my lawfully wedded husband and me. And, God have mercy on your *demented* soul, you actually had the gumption to punish my niece by forcing her to miss recess and write a lot of completely irresponsible and unethical stuff based on *your* religious beliefs. No ma'am, you most certainly did *not* tell my niece the truth."

Thoroughly disgusted and having worked up a full head of steam, I turned my attention back to the principal. "I will ask you again, Principal Johnson, what you intend to do about this situation, because clearly neither Allen nor I will let this incompetent and immoral woman be alone with *our* nieces again."

I sat silently while the man visibly squirmed in front of us.

"I will need to speak to the superintendent," he said.

"Good, then you should let them know our attorney will be in contact with you."

I stood and Allen stood with me. Before we could leave, the horrible woman said, "You are damaging those poor innocent girls. You should be ashamed."

"Your opinion is irrelevant, but especially considering all that's happened to those girls in the past few months, I can positively assure you that the only person here who should be ashamed is you!"

We left then, and Allen drove as I basically fell apart in the passenger seat. The emotions of the past few days swept over me as I came to terms with those poor girls being forced to feel what I'd felt all those years ago, that they weren't part of our family, and that they could lose us at any moment.

I'd never forgive the hateful woman for making them feel that way, especially after they'd lost so much already.

Fifty

Allen

Mom found an attorney who worked with the American Civil Liberties Union on similar cases, and we retained him the following day. The attorney quickly informed us that the school district had decided not to condemn what the teacher had said or done.

It only took a couple of moments after hearing that for us to ask him to press charges. We wouldn't let the school treat kids of gay parents that way. Not now, not ever.

That's when we officially took the kids out of school. They'd been through sheer hell the past year, losing their parents, then their home, and now their new school and any friends they'd made. At least they only had a few weeks left in the school year anyway. We figured they could enroll again in the fall, and it sure as hell wouldn't be in the same school district.

Mom had already offered to let us live in her over-the-top palace in Franklin, and we were seriously considering it. I knew Mom was renovating it to sell, but we'd need a place for the girls to go to school next fall if we remained in the area, and Franklin was known for having an excellent and much more tolerant school system.

We were in Martha's Vineyard with the girls, Alexi and Fiona, when our attorney called and said the school wanted to settle out of court. When news of the case had hit the media, it began to spread like wildfire, and the school decided it would rather mitigate as much damage as possible.

Ultimately, they fired the teacher, and agreed to make an official complaint to the state board of education against the teacher's license. They also agreed to have all the staff in the district go through sensitivity training.

It was about as perfect an outcome as we could've hoped. That being said, I'd never expose the girls to that school district ever again. When I said as much to Gib, he readily agreed.

Both Fiona and Alexi tried to talk us into leaving Tennessee and coming to the Northeast, where it was much more gay-friendly in general.

"No, Tennessee might not be perfect, but it's home and it'll never change unless people stand up to the bigots. Unless something happens, we're gonna stick to it out there," I said to them all.

The girls were fine or mostly fine. Despite our best efforts and weeks of therapy with Jan, they still had fears of being taken away. Jan had advised us that time was the only thing that would prove to the girls that the old biddy was wrong.

Time, we had. At least I hoped we did.

I knew deep down I wasn't going anywhere. I loved my job, and my peers and colleagues seemed to like me. My fears of not being accepted were unfounded. I might not have graduated from there, but I'd been there long enough that I'd become one of them.

When Gib interviewed for a family physician job in a small town just east of Nashville called Crawford City, I rolled my eyes. He really was a small-town boy.

At first, Gib wasn't overly excited about the job. "It's in a part of the state where Nashville still has a lot of influence, but it's super rural." We both had a bad taste in our mouths after the massive fuck-up at the last school for extremely rural not to sound all that appealing.

Before he interviewed for the position, the girls, Gib, and I had driven over to the town to check it out.

Cute. That was my first impression. Small, likely built in the Victorian era, and pretty typical for a Southern railroad town.

We stopped at a restaurant that served home cooking. The place was packed, but everyone was friendly, even when it was clear that Gib and I were a couple.

"What do you think?" Gib asked when we piled back into the car. The girls were bickering in the back, which usually meant they didn't care one way or the other.

"I like it, I guess. But it's pretty similar to where we were before," I said, feeling less than happy about the memories of the school.

When we drove down a beautiful tree-lined street with a park on either side, the girls looked out just in time to see a large Victorian home right in front of us. "Look," Chrissy said, with more enthusiasm than I'd heard from her in a long time. "It looks like our house."

She was right. The Victorian they'd grown up in was almost exactly the same as this one. I thought they called it Queen Anne style. The front porch was a little larger than theirs had been, though. I'd guess the whole house was probably a little bigger, but of course, that could be because it sat on a slight hill above the downtown area.

Gib smiled at the beautiful old home as we drove by. "When they get the museum up and running in our old house, we'll go back and see what all they did with it," he said, more to himself than the girls. When I looked in the rearview mirror, I saw mixed feelings in the girls' expressions.

Instead of saying anything, I reached over and squeezed my husband's hand.

FIFTY-ONE

GIB

I WAS SKEPTICAL ABOUT the job, until I walked in and saw how slammed the little clinic was. As far as I could tell, Dr. Nash was the only provider there, and patients were waiting in the lobby. Everyone seemed to be content to sit in the waiting room, or maybe they were just used to it. Some coughed while the older ones complained about this or that.

I'd worn my white jacket, thinking it would be appropriate, since I basically refused to wear a suit jacket in the intense heat.

The older patients homed in on me like a fly to poo. Within seconds of Dr. Nash telling me he wouldn't have time to see me for a while, patients began telling me their symptoms. Some went into such detail that I became uncomfortable with our public situation.

I went to the front desk and asked the woman manning it if there was a more private place where I could speak with some of the regulars, just so they wouldn't be airing their ailments to the general public.

The receptionist, who introduced herself as Clara Sue, smiled in a harried way and led me to an office that looked as if it hadn't been used in over ten years. I quickly went back out and gestured to one of the patients who had disclosed to me that she'd been having heartburn.

I figured she was one of the clinic's frequent-flyers, and sure enough, the more she told me, the more I saw that Dr. Nash had done all he could for her. "It seems to me you're being treated about as well as can be expected," I said. "Sometimes it just takes a while for things to kick in." I checked her vitals and didn't observe anything she wasn't already being treated for.

The woman nodded happily, and left without setting up another appointment. As I suspected, she just needed to know she was still doing the right thing.

I was about to go back out and wait myself when another elderly patient came up and gestured me back to the little room. I almost laughed out loud at how the patients seemed to be controlling me, and I had yet to even have an interview.

He had lost his wife a few months before and overcome cancer just a couple years before that. I let him talk for several moments, and was about to tell him he probably should see Dr. Nash before he left, when he said, "I see him every week. He just says the same thing over and over again."

"It sounds like Doctor Nash has given you some sound advice," I finally said, and the old man smiled from ear to ear.

"That's a comfort to know, son," he said as he stood to go.

He left chipper as could be, telling Clara Sue that he'd see her Monday.

"Martha, you should see this young man. He's smart, like our Doctor Nash!" he said to a woman sitting in a wheelchair next to the entrance.

"You'll do then," she said as she began wheeling her way back through the side door. I looked at Clara Sue, who was trying not to smile. When she made eye contact, she winked at me and I shrugged, letting her know I didn't know what was going on.

One of Martha's legs had been amputated above the knee, and she had a small bite on the underside of her stump. She said she had diabetes, and was concerned that a mosquito bite might cause issues.

"I'd say you should get the opinion of a doctor who works here," I said, starting to feel very uncomfortable that three patients had sought my feedback. I wasn't even employed here, and although I certainly wasn't offering any medical advice, I was toeing a fine line.

"Is that gonna give me problems or not?" she asked, and I shrugged.

"I doubt it. Don't you want to see Doctor Nash?" I asked.

"No, he's too busy today. I'll come back on Monday. When are you going to start? I swear that poor man works day and night over the likes of me."

I chuckled. "I have to be interviewed first."

Dr. Nash and I came out at the same time Martha waved at him as she left. He looked at me skeptically. "Did you see patients?" he asked.

"No," I chuckled. "When the patients you had waiting saw my doctor's coat, they began telling me all their symptoms, so I asked if Clara Sue could give us a private place to talk. I didn't offer any medical advice, but it seems these were your frequent-fliers anyway. I listened and by the time I was done, they all decided they could wait until Monday to see you."

That made Dr. Nash chuckle. "You catch on quick. Well, seeing as you've cleaned me out of patients, let's go back to my office and chat."

We sat down together, and I explained I'd done my residency in a health center, and that I wanted to work in a rural area that wasn't too far from Nashville. We needed to be close because of Allen's job at the hospital.

"Why, with a Harvard degree, wouldn't you want to work in a more prestigious place?" he asked.

There it was, the issue I figured would have to be explained again and again. "I went to Harvard, but I'm from a small town in West Tennessee. I love my hometown, but now that I've got three children, I'd prefer to raise them in a more accepting place. If you decide to hire me, my family can move between here and Nashville, where my husband works. We want to give our kids a good place to go to school, and still not have to drive hours to work."

"Sounds like a plan. How long do you plan to stay in Tennessee?" he asked.

"I doubt I'll move," I answered. "This is home."

"Well, in that case, welcome aboard. When can you start?"

"How about next week?" I asked, clearly surprising him. I wasn't going to let the opportunity pass. It was perfect for what I wanted to do, it was close to Nashville, and the town seemed quaint.

"That's soon. Don't you have to give notice?"

"No," I chuckled. "After my residency, I worked at the clinic for a while, until we had a family tragedy. I had to spend more time with the girls while they settled. The clinic was able to replace me, so I've been volunteering until I accept a permanent position."

"Which town are you considering moving to?" he asked.

When I said Mayville, a town we'd come through on the way here, he winced. "I don't mean to be discouraging, but that town is not friendly to gay men, and you said you have a husband and are raising three children. There's a preacher there that'll make your lives miserable, I'm afraid."

I sighed. "I was afraid of that. I still need to do some research. The small town I grew up in had quite a few of those preachers, and the town is basically run by the religious university there, so even though it's pretty open now, it's still not the best place for us to raise our kids."

"I'll tell you what, since you freed my morning up, I'll take you around Crawford City. It's small, but it's about as open to our kind of folks as any small rural town in Tennessee can be. Besides, it's just a little over half an hour's drive to Nashville. It might be worth it to move here and have your husband commute."

I thought about it. "Well, it's not like he hasn't had that kind of commute before. He and I have been commuting that far since we started our residencies. I'll ask him what he thinks."

"Well, when I show you the Cross house, he might be more enticed. She and her sister lived there for over ninety years. Miss Cross went into the nursing home last month, and her great-nephew is about to put the place up for sale."

We walked over to the same diner we'd eaten at when Allen, the girls, and I had driven here to check it out. Dr. Nash ordered us to-go sandwiches, which we ate as we walked past the town hall and through a city park before coming to Cross Street.

"This is also known as Lover's Lane since kids were known to park along the parkway making out all hours of the night," Dr. Nash was saying as I spotted the Queen Anne home, and literally gasped.

"For real? This is the home you wanted to show me?"

Dr. Nash chuckled. "Yep, and it's in impeccable shape. Both the Cross sisters were amateur carpenters, so the home never went without regular maintenance."

"Can we see it?"

"Let me call Danny and see if he minds us going in."

I looked at him, shocked. "You've got the keys?"

He shook his head, laughing. "Um, no, that house hasn't been locked since it was built. The sisters were heavily involved in youth leadership programs, especially those relating to agriculture, so basically every kid in town went in and out of there for meetings over the years. Besides, Danny Cross, the Cross sisters' great-nephew, is also married to the county sheriff, Pat Cross, and everyone is too scared to do anything that might get her dander up."

I shook my head. "I mean, I'm from a small town myself, but this is a bit out there even for me."

He chuckled. "Welcome to Crawford City."

We'd just gone into the house when Dr. Nash was called back to the clinic to deal with a patient. He told me to wander around and to give Danny a call directly if I had questions. After saving Danny's number in my phone, Dr. Nash headed back to the clinic.

I walked through the beautiful old home, and although it was similar to the Victorian, there were very distinct differences. The most noticeable was the elegant mahogany paneling along the walls, the enormous crown molding in the parlor, and beautiful art deco light fixtures that sparkled, but were clearly not installed until the twenties or thirties.

The old Victorian I grew up in was nowhere near as opulent as this one, but there were enough similarities that this place still felt like home, and I knew the girls would settle into it perfectly as well.

When I went into the retro kitchen, though, I almost backed out. It was so ugly and out of place in this beautiful mansion.

So, it needs a few changes. Entirely doable.

I wandered up the stairs and couldn't help but laugh. The second floor was almost exactly the same as the home I'd grown up in. The rooms were slightly bigger, but the overall layout was identical.

I went back downstairs and phoned Allen. When he picked up, I said, "I think I've found our forever home."

"Really? Where?" he asked.

"Do you remember the beautiful old mansion at the end of that park in Crawford City?" I asked him.

"Yeah."

"Well, I'm sitting in the formal living room right now. It's beyond gorgeous, Allen, and from what I can tell, it's in impeccable shape."

"The house the girls called home?" he asked. "It's for sale?"

"Yep, can you pick the girls up from your mom's and meet me here?" I asked.

"Yes. In fact, hell yes. Oh, did you take the job then?"

"Oh, sorry, yeah, I should've led with that. It's the perfect job. Perfect town, perfect job, and apparently Doctor Nash plays for our team."

"You lucky dog, just make sure he knows you're already tied up with me and three girls."

"I think that's pretty clear, since I wouldn't shut up about you all."

I could hear his soft laughter before he got pulled away. "I'll finish up here, then go get the girls. See you in a couple hours."

"I love you, Allen."

"I love you too, sweetheart."

I wandered around the old home again, looking at all the living spaces, imagining what we'd have to do to make it more our style. I liked how a home like this offered plenty of spaces to crawl into to read a book, or just be alone with your thoughts. I'd appreciated that growing up in the old Victorian, and I wanted that for the girls here.

I quickly took a picture of the exterior and texted Miss Margaret, telling her we were looking. When I almost did the same to Chase and Olivia's phone numbers, I felt my world quake a bit. It'd been a while since I'd nearly texted them, and even now, it still undid me.

I was feeling nostalgic. I couldn't believe how lucky we were to find this house that already felt like our home. I hadn't even called Danny yet to find out the listing price. Hopefully, it wouldn't be too expensive, but unless it was ridiculous, I figured with the money in my trust, along with the money we got from the sale of the old house to the historical society, we'd be able to make it work.

Between Allen's support, the girls' reaction to the house when we'd driven by, and the glowing feedback Miss Margaret texted back, I knew I had to make a move on the property. So, I called Danny Cross to ask if it was okay to visit the house again that night with my family in tow.

"Sure, just make sure you turn off the lights when you're done."

"Mr. Cross, I should probably ask the price."

It was fortunate we were on the phone, because when he told me, my jaw just about dropped. The price was half what I thought it would be. "I'm pretty sure we're your buyer, but as I said, my husband and nieces need to see it."

"My great-aunt will be pleased that it's going to a family," he said. "It's always had children running through those halls, but for the past fifty years, it's been the community's kids."

"Well, I'll give you a call when we have an answer for you," I said, feeling emotional over the kid comment. I wasn't exactly sure why, except the place reminded me so much of my home growing up.

When I got back to the clinic, the place only had a few patients left, so I spent some time talking to the receptionist, Clara Sue.

Dr. Nash saw his last two patients, then Clara Sue put the closed sign up and returned to her desk to finish her duties for the day. Dr. Nash plopped down next to me and smiled.

"I have no words to say how much I appreciated your help today. I swear, if you hadn't come in, I'd still be dealing with patients. Yesterday I was here until after seven."

I chuckled. "The life we've chosen, huh?"

He shook his head. "What were we thinking?"

"So, my husband is bringing the girls out to see the house. Would you like to grab supper while I wait?"

He thought for a moment and smiled. "Two meals together in one day? If your husband wasn't coming, the gossip would get so ripe we could pick it."

I chuckled again. "I'll make sure the hubby and girls meet us at the diner then. He has a tendency toward PDA, so there'll be no question who I belong to when they arrive."

Dr. Nash rushed back to finish up his paperwork. Clara Sue put me to work helping finish up the evening routine, which I couldn't help but laugh at. This was exactly the kind of work environment I wanted, where everyone pitched in when work needed doing, regardless of their job title.

Dr. Nash came out, and while Clara Sue locked up and walked toward her car, he and I walked to the Crawford City Café for the second time that day. The sandwiches we'd eaten earlier were good, but the evening buffet was to die for. Food that was reminiscent of dishes prepared by some of the best cooks from my hometown was sitting along the buffet line like a banquet of happiness.

"Do you mind if I go ahead and announce that you're gonna be our new doctor?" Dr. Nash asked.

I smiled. "Sure, might as well get the gossip mill working. That way, when I come to work, I'll be able to jump right in."

"You should know that you've already met the town's most notorious gossips, and I don't just mean my receptionist. Just letting them spew their ailments like you did means you'll be so busy the day you arrive, you'll be lucky to see daylight before Christmas."

I couldn't help but laugh. We continued chatting about the clinic and the community as we piled our buffet plates high.

The café was intense. There was so much gossiping between the tables around us, I almost wanted to film it so I could send it to Fiona and Alexi. They'd never believe it was really like this unless they saw it for themselves.

Dr. Nash finally rolled his eyes, and whispered, "Might as well get the show on the road," before he cleared his throat, and loudly said, "Doctor McCartney, when you take on your position at the clinic, you'll want to get a daily punch card here. It's saved me a pile of money."

It was as if the entire place sighed at once. As the gossip subsided, people began coming over to introduce themselves to me.

When we had a moment to ourselves, Dr. Nash smiled and shook his head. "So, you still wanna work here?"

I laughed. "More than ever."

Two striking older men walked up then with an incredibly handsome younger man between them. I could tell by how much two of them looked alike that they were father and son. As soon as Dr. Nash saw them, he smiled hesitantly. "Hey, Dad, meet Doctor Gibbon McCartney." When I shook the older man's hand, he grinned.

"I'm glad to see you. So, have you decided to take over my old position?" he asked.

I smiled and nodded. "I accepted the job today. I'll start next week."

"Ah, that's good news. My son has been begging me to come out of retirement, which I've refused, of course. Maybe he'll leave me alone now. You can call me Doc, everyone else does. This is Amos, and that one is Todd."

I smiled at the brooding man and gave a half-wave. I wasn't sure why, but it felt like the guy could fillet me in seconds and serve me up for supper. When I turned to look at Dr. Nash, I had an aha moment. There was something going on between them.

I looked up just in time to see Allen and the girls come in the front door. I stood and waved at them, and they made a beeline toward me.

"Uncle Gib," Chrissy said, all excited. "We were at the railroad and a train came down it. The conductor waved at us and honked his horn."

Allen leaned over and kissed me possessively on the lips. *Jealous much*, I thought, but didn't say anything.

Allen had told me he'd be stopping to get the girls' supper, so there was no need to stick around the café. There was just a little daylight left, and I wanted them to see the house before it got too dark.

The second we drove up to the house, the girls squealed. "Uncle Allen, you didn't tell us it was this house!" Chrissy said.

I almost felt myself get emotional again before I reined it in. We'd all shed so many tears already, and I wanted this moment to be a happy memory for them.

FIFTY-TWO

ALLEN

THE HOUSE REALLY WAS perfect... enormous, but perfect. Gib and I wandered around and the girls decided to do their own exploration. "Just don't touch anything," Gib said as they took off on their own.

"What do you think?" Gib asked.

"I think it's perfect. How much is it?"

He smiled and told me the price. "No way! Why is it so cheap?"

"'Cause, we're in the middle of nowhere," Gib replied.

"Can we get a contract on it now, before someone else snatches it away? I mean, seriously, it's not that far from Nashville."

Gib just smiled as we continued walking through the house. "This is really the only bad part of it," he said, and led me into the kitchen. It was spotless, but dang, it looked straight out of a nineteen-fifties magazine.

"Yeah, if it was a museum, sure, but this will have to go," I said, trying not to scrunch my nose up.

The girls had all picked their own bedrooms before we even made it upstairs. Of course, poor Chrissy had chosen the master bedroom as her own, but Gib and I shut down that idea quickly. "Let's go up and see if the attic is like the old home was. If so, you could get that room since you're the oldest," I said, trying to assuage her obvious disappointment.

Luckily, the attic was usable space, and someone had renovated it, albeit in what looked to be the sixties. Hopefully, there'd be insulation in the renovation, because I could just imagine what the steamy nights of summer and frigid nights of winter would feel like in there otherwise.

Chrissy looked rather disgusted at the room. "It'll need new paint, and we'll get you some new carpet from this decade. When it's done it'll be perfect, you'll see," Gib said, sounding downright chipper.

She wasn't convinced, but there were plenty of bedrooms on the second level if she wasn't. She'd just have to share a bathroom with her sisters.

We walked down to the gardens as the sun set, enjoying the beauty in the twilight.

"I think I love it here," I said, and the smile that had never left Gib's face brightened.

"Wanna call to make an offer now?" he asked.

"Of course!" I said. An hour later, we'd met the great-nephew, who had power of attorney over the place, and signed the contract. In the end, we'd also inherited all the antique furniture and kitschy odds and ends the family had insisted stay with the house.

Gib sighed heavily when we heard that. Later, as we were about to leave for home, he said he'd grown up with that sort of uncomfortable stuff, and had no intention of living with it now.

"Maybe we can have an auction or donate it or something."

"Maybe," he said hesitantly, then his smile returned. "I'm so excited!"

Chrissy hugged him and it was clear she was excited as well. I liked the old home. It wouldn't have been my first choice, since I thought of myself as more of a modern architecture lover, but it wasn't any sort of sacrifice, seeing how happy the house made the rest of my family. They were my home and that was all I needed.

Fifty-Three

Epilogue: Allen

THE TRANSITION INTO OUR new home was easier than I would've ever imagined. We launched into making updates to it while preparing to sell our other house. Todd, the guy who was dating Gib's boss, Dr. Nash, was an extremely gifted contractor, and he and his crew replaced the kitchen, updated the bathrooms, gave Chrissy's attic bedroom a facelift, insulated the house, and replaced the upstairs windows with energy efficient ones.

I sold the other house the day I listed it to the daughter of one of our neighbors. She'd wanted to buy it when I had, but was still in school at the time. Having since graduated, she now had a husband and one-year-old son and wanted to live close to her parents, so they could help out with their grandchild.

The elementary school in Crawford City was much better than the bigoted one the girls were in before, so much so that all three were excited for school every day.

Everything was going smoothly, until Todd told us he was renovating an old building located along the defunct railroad tracks, and converting it into a boutique hotel.

I wasn't sure what got into me, but before I knew it, I told him I'd invest in it with him. I'd never been interested in owning a hotel, but something about the old building and its beautiful wood beams spoke to me. Plus, I was hook, line, and sinker—as Gib liked to say—in love with my new hometown and wanted to be a part of it.

I'd already made several friends, including Dr. Nash and Todd, not to mention their fathers, who were a newlywed couple themselves. I loved their story of love and how they'd held out until now, but never gave up on one another.

I'd also met a couple of gay guys who were starting a winery. I didn't see them often, but one was an artist and I really liked some of his work. I knew I lived in a Victorian that still retained some of the antique furniture we'd been saddled with, but I could envision some of his abstract art hanging on the walls of the old home.

In moving to this quaint town and joining a community that'd fully accepted our family, life was finally where I wanted it to be. I was happier than I thought I'd ever been. I had a loving husband, three beautiful girls, a mom who I'd never been closer to, a fulfilling job, and caring friends. Tragedy had hit us hard, and it was still hard at times, but we'd work through it and anything else that came our way together... as a family.

Facing the past is never fun, especially when it involves seeing the man you still love. When their lives are once again intertwined, is a second chance possible? Continue the Coming Home Series with ***Family Home***

Available at your favorite bookseller.

Join Blake's email list to get advance notice of new books and receive his occasional newsletter:

www.blakeallwood.com

MM Romance By Blake Allwood	Romantic Fantasy By Adam J. Ridley

MM Romance
By Blake Allwood

Transitions Series
Aiden Inspired
Suzie Empowered (MF Romance)
Bobby Transformed

Chance Series
Love By Chance
Another Chance With Love
Taking A Chance For Love

Romantic Series
Romantic Renovations (1)
Romantic Rescue (2)
Romantic Recon (3)

Melody Series
Melody of the Heart
Melody of the Snow

Road to Rocktoberfest Anthology
Changing His Tune - 2022

Coming Home Series (2023)
A Long Way Home
Family Home
Down Home
…and many more

Novellas
Tenacious
Moon's Place

Romantic Fantasy
By Adam J. Ridley

Big Bend Series
Love's Legacy (1)
Love's Heirloom (2)
Love's Bequest (3)

The Witch Brothers Series
Emerald Earth
Diamond Air
Ruby Fire
Sapphire Water

Blake Allwood was born in west Tennessee, then moved to Kansas City MO after earning a degree in Early Childhood Education from Graceland College in Lamoni, Iowa. He met his husband Shaun in 1995 and they officially married in 2015, once gay marriage was legalized; although they still consider Valentines Day 1995 as their true "anniversary date". Twenty-two years later (2017), after fostering 12 children together, he and his husband sold their home, purchased an RV and began traveling the country with their two dogs.

Typically, Blake can be found relaxing in the RV or by the fire with his laptop and their Jack Russell Terrier, Buddy, curled up between his legs demanding attention. Denver, their Siberian Husky mix is often asleep at his feet or playing tug of war with Blake's husband.

Blake also writes under the pen name of Adam J. Ridley for his romantic fantasy and urban fantasy readers looking for stories revolving around gay characters. His first series is The Witch Brothers Saga, starting with ***Emerald Earth***.

BIBLIOPRIDE.COM

Books by LGBTQ+ Authors